 Santiago Martinez Concha

MIEL

Santiago Martínez Concha

Santiago Martinez Concha

I

The night Jacob had his first experience with the angel Miel he woke up crying, he saw when a jagged sword went through his body as if it was made of melted wax, it went through the mattress, the bed tables that served as support and ended up crashing into the room's wooden floor. First, he heard a thud and tried to stand up but it was impossible. He was nailed like an insect to a piece of cork, he could see the being on his bed's left side holding the sword and he felt a deep physical pain when the air escaped out his lungs and a crying like the howl of a wounded dog escaped through his throat. After a moment, summoning all his strength he asked:

—Who… are you?

—I'm Miel—, he said bluntly—, I've many names. Don't be afraid! I live in the breeze, so a gentle wind always follows me and my eyes are like two shining drops of honey glowing after dark. I'll give you a few days to find your destiny, you've been idle for too long!

—How do you expect me to do that? He asked frighten and in deep pain.

—Don't be afraid! Fear is a disease of the soul and only faith can cure it. I'll be your guide in the sea of your memories. You'll have to traverse the spiral of time where each passing day, things will become clearer. Some of the memories you never experienced them, they happened before you existed, and they were inherited from your father's words, but they are also part of you. Be grateful for this opportunity! Gratitude is the memory of the heart!

It was three o'clock in the morning. Despite the pain, Jacob felt a deep pleasure throughout the encounter. The strange creature had eyes like two drops of liquid crystal resembling two drops of honey glowing in the dark. The angel seemed to float over the floor, he wore sandals with leather straps holding them around his ankle. His gown, made of fine silk with red flashes moved freely in the room's quiet air, the rest of his clothes showed bluish overtones. A brooch with gold arabesques held his tunic, and formed a spiral with its rays that went out in all directions; Jacob looked ecstatic. He'd never seen a creature so strange and beautiful before. His words sounded like an echo of his own conscience.

The creature held a sword in his hands stuck at that moment in Jacob chest. His arms were covered with a transparent veil of delicate brocades. He looked calm and compassionate at the same time, his ivory skin, as taken from an old painting by Caravaggio, illuminated from inside. Then Jacob asked breathlessly:

—What is the meaning of the talisman, flaunting in the middle of your chest?

—It's the spiral of life, going in circles around its centre where the heart of life exists. Always expanding, always growing. The same applies to history and time. Galaxies and all living beings copy it and they are formed like it. Henceforth, you'll write about all you live and see. Let others judge your flaws and virtues, every human being is made of both. The problem arises when the balance is broken; so, it's necessary to take an honest inventory and review your steps. Don't be afraid, your world is sinking in chaos, the poets have died and nobody can help you except me.

—And ... for what reason you just gave me a few days?

—Most healers advise even more time, but in your case, a few days are enough. Be thankful and let go of all your past! Following the instructions of someone more powerful than me I'm about to change your destiny. You'll have to accept the pain of growing up and you'll be remade in the crucible of the brave. You'll never be the same, are you ready?

—I'm not a coward. I know many of my faults and shortcomings, some I like others I don't… I'm used to them… Not sure if I want or I can change them. I don't even know where to begin...

—Start by anyone, it doesn't matter. The small defects lead to the large and the large lead to the small. Do you know what's the greatest of them?

—I have too many! It's not an easy task…

—Knowledge is a good start, honesty an indispensable tool and fear is a blockade; you must overcome fears through faith… Now, tell me some…

Still with the bittersweet pain induced by the sword he spoke gasping:

—I think I'm selfish, lustful, impatient and proud. The problem is that I've learned to disguise my shortcomings with masks that show me as being generous, pious, humble, and provided with a great behaviour, but deep inside myself, I know that's not true. I envy people who know how to give themselves to others without expecting anything in return; I was born like those; somewhere hidden within me I feel I'm still like that. I simply misplaced the map of my return. Unfortunately, the day after my father died, I lost my innocence and bit of the forbidden fruit, I was never the same after that. Since then there is something inside me that blocks the path of true love, keeping me away from happiness, a few days to change may not be enough…

—Maybe, maybe not... it depends on you. You gave the first step tonight. In life's spiral there is no return, what you did you did, but you can make amends to yourself and others and redirect your path. Begin now crossing the desert of your life. Soon you'll come to the "'Y" where the path splits. Be careful not to choose the wrong path this time, you could lose everything! Hurry! Run! Don't waste time! The clock is ticking! Your destination is buried deep within the roots of the Big Tree.

—Big Tree?

—Yes, some call it the Tree of Life ... If your name is not written in it, you'll never arrive to the happy destiny the Great Designer had prepared for you.

—Great Designer?

—Yes, others call Him God or use many other names to refer to Him, but it all accounts to the same.

—tell me more about the Big Tree…

—Ancient books mention it. Written in its roots are all your actions, memories, thoughts, feelings, virtues and defects, everything you've experienced and what you still need to live. When I'll come back to visit you again, we'll talk about it. From now on you must learn to discern. One thing will be your life during a day time and another at night. You're still divided in two halves, one is black and the other is the white, but you're missing the greys. Remember… don't look for the truth only in the extremes of the arch made by the pendulum's swing. The truth exists also along the way… don't miss the grey scale.

—It all sounds too complicated for me.

—You'll understand more as time passes. I must go now. Someone else urgently needs my help. With the first rays of the sun I'll vanish into thin air…

He felt the tip of the sword deep into his body

scavenging for his bowels, and then the creature withdrew the sword with them hanging, entangled in the end. Before departing, he looked at Jacob for a couple of seconds in a mixture of compassion and goodwill, and then started to fade slowly as if vapour mist, leaving no trace. Jacob put his hands on his chest and then on his belly trying to find out if his heart was still beating or his bowels were there. He wasn't sure. Though his heart had been pierced set an even pace, but his bowels he saw them disappear crimped at the tip of the creature's sword that came from elsewhere.

Breathing with difficulty, bathed in his own sweat and tears as the last witnesses of his experience, he rose from his bed and making an effort went to an old wooden table that served him, depending on the occasion, for dinning or for writing. On top was a big box. He opened it and began a frantic search. For years he buried in it all that passed through his hands and didn't know how to get rid of. It was an extension of his life. Broken lighters, dead batteries, nuts that didn't fit in any screw, faceless cards, a pocket radio he bought in one of his trips and never used, a box camera that once belonged to his father, pictures from when he was younger, women's photos of those who passed through his life, useless pens and eyeglasses who lacked a glass. In the bottom he found what he sought: the perfumed little sandal box inherited from his mother filled with various images he collected as a child. In one of them there was an identical angel to the one he just saw; observed him for a long time, without missing a single detail, remembering everything he'd lived that same night.

Across the street, a sinister owl watched him silently from its nest in the old oak tree, it represented the darkness he once lived and the danger if he slipped back into his old ways, being there as the only witness of his last experience, but Jacob didn't notice it. With his remaining strength, following Miel's instructions he started to search his memory, looking for clues from his past. With great effort, began writing about his experience and managed to calm his soul.

The first memories he recalled were the words inherited from his father. Before his birth, Vincent looked for a name in an old dictionary that survived a public burning in the middle of a town square. He felt by doing so, somehow rescued shrouded in smoke from the huge fire, the body of that ancient monk, being tied to a stake by order of that sacrilegious pope who condemned him to die in flames. A pope excommunicated by the same monk, who courageously denounced the orgies and excesses of the flesh of a church lost in the labyrinths of its own sins. The monk waited patiently since then to be included one day in the calendar of saints. Vincent felt that after five hundred years, his spirit was still alive and that somehow, he was the living witness of his teachings, deciding to pass that legacy to his only son. What he didn't know was when and how he'd meet his own death.

Vincent was an educated man who at one time took the decision to travel like a gypsy breaking with his past; selling everything he had, he bought a wagon, he took his wife with him and began reciting along roadsides and remote villages, Milton's, Lorca's, Carol's, Quevedo's, Machado's, Byron's, Neruda's, Keats', Octavio Paz' and Borges' poems, an activity that allowed him to survive. Often thought about differences between heroes and martyrs, but in the end, all ended up being the useful idiots of a society seeking only to serve its own selfish purposes. Experience showed him that very few truly sacrificed for others. Generosity and humility both preached from pulpits, for him were empty words that seldom found a true echo among the faithful ones. The aberrations of some clergy cried to heaven with scandals. He'd read somewhere that the hands of those consecrated to God, leading the faithful people to abandon the faith by their example, they would burn in hell with a special flame. He pictured it like a pale blue colour produced by a voltaic arc applied to the raw flesh, burning eternally without ever turning it off.

Often thought of eternity as a word he associated with infinity, a never-ending process of adding one second to the next; thinking how small he was in the universe's immensity and these thoughts always lead him to think in God. He liked the idea of becoming a martyr to be remembered with admiration, but was no longer used to be crucified or burn to death, and he didn't know if when the time came, he'd have the strength to stand firm on his beliefs. What remained of the once evil Inquisition were some obsolete courts which very few cared about it! He often thought about the 'mother church' he loved versus the 'stepmother church' which he abhorred. But what he didn't know was that his fear of being embraced by flames would be justified over time.

Moving his fingertips over the book's charred edges, he decided for a name blurred by centuries. It was not one of saints nor one of apostles. For some reason when he thought about it, a swallow crossing his path dropped its excrement landing in a star's form on the book's cover. Vincent felt it was an omen and that the name he'd chosen was confirmed. Maybe his son would have the seed of a true philosopher, a historian, a warrior, a poet, a hero or the martyr he'd always wanted to be. Unfortunately, his talent was only enough to recite verses of others with impeccable diction. Although his words were swept by a dry desert's wind, wrapped in clouds of dust, the memory of a peculiar hiss produced by his white teeth box hidden behind a thick moustache was still in the memory of those who once heard him.

Somehow a Hebrew name would be appropriate.

At eight months pregnant he told Ruth his intentions, his wife for more than a decade. She, knowing about her husband's stubbornness and accepting beforehand all the reasons given to her, decided not to contradict him in his endeavour. On her part, she'd baptize him secretly in her heart calling him Ramón, in memory of the man who wrote the only book she ever read and mourn from the moment she opened it.

The simple christening ceremony was planned to be performed by the village's parish priest of a town lost on its own misery, where the children covered by crusts of dust clay resembled mud sculptures. The spiral of destiny began to turn faster from the moment the child was born. Ruth pictured him with a mission in life. One thing for another, perhaps her incredible pain would help the child to bear it when it came... He might become a great healer, or perhaps a poet. In the first thing, she was right. In the second, too.

When the priest out of curiosity pursued the woman's cries brought by the wind, he reached the wagon on the side of the road parked under a huge oak, he saw an intense blue light coming from inside illuminate the mare's back and the stones on the road and interpreted this as a sign from heaven. With a leap slipped under the wagon's canvas and he saw Vincent washing the baby in a fresh water bowl stained with blood. He saw when he cut the umbilical cord with the scissors which help him prune the mare that pulled his wagon and his fate. The blue light illuminated the interior showing the faces of those present as if they were not of this world. Then something else happened. A swallow slipped into the wagon and stood at the bed's edge where Ruth made her labour. Other two soon followed and stood beside the first. A few seconds later others came under the canvas and landed on every corner that might accommodate them. Vincent and the priest were perplexed. At first, they wanted to scare them, but Ruth begged to let them stay. Then she spoke in a clear voice in a mixture of tiredness and pain.

—It's a miracle...! A miracle! Don't you see? Let them

be here! I think it's a sign from heaven... They came to take me—.
And then she fainted.

—Soon! Vincent cried to the priest—. Help me! She's
dying... Help me!

The priest took the crucifix hidden in his robe and
began to recite Latin litanies required by the rite of extreme
unction. At that moment Ruth opened her eyes and said:

—Baptize him now; you've to snatch him from the
devil!

—And how do you want to call him?

—Jacob of the Blessed Sacrament Juan Ramón of the
Swallows...

The priest turned his head to Vincent and he agreed to
it. Once finished with the rite of extreme unction and anointing the
forehead, hands and feet with oil from a bottle also hidden in
another pocket of his cassock, continued with the rite of baptism,
while the swallows, she and Vincent watched in silence.

Ruth died shortly after. A serene smile imprinted in her
face. Vincent's tears bathed her hands while holding them in
his. But those tears would also purify his destination and his
child's, marking their paths like a stones' rosary, with a mysterious
purpose ...

Vincent stayed with his son, fulfilling the mission of
father-mother which destiny had entrusted him; flocks of swallows
and other birds ever abandoning them. Soon became accustomed to
its presence. No matter what time of the year, they were always
watching every move they made. Everywhere they went, the
swallows were taking turns accompanying them in their doings and
if they strayed too far from its nests, others came and settled on the
wagon's canvas. Vincent interpreted all this as a sign from heaven,
establishing a mysterious link at the time of birth between his child

and the birds, a link that would emerge over time. The days passed and time proved him right. A strange thing happened. Jacob with only two years of age one day whistled. It was a beautiful hiss, like music coming from the heart and in it, Vincent thought he recognized the words

'Father... father, Jacob... here I'm'.

As days went by the child began to whistle more and more. Despite his father's efforts he failed to teach him how to pronounce a single word, although, in the whistles he recognized some of the verses he recited. Vincent was publicly ashamed that his son could not speak, but secretly rejoiced he could whistle with such skill. Maybe one day he'd articulate some words. At first, he thought, Jacob was held by a spell caused by the name chosen and blamed himself for it, but soon he found out that more than a curse was a blessing. The child grew up healthy and strong as the oak covering the wagon at the moment of his birth. At age of four he could whistle four consonants and six vowels combining them in a thousand different ways, but incredibly enough, his language was understandable to anyone who'd listen. At age of six, staring for a moment at the sun, he whistled excitedly:

—*I saw my mother! I saw my mother*—! Vincent alarmed by the whistles ran towards him and rebuked him in amazement:

—That's impossible! Your mother died when you were born, I've told you before...! The dead are dead, although they see us from the sky through a window that opens when we pray for them—... Then the boy whistled again.

—No matter what you say, I saw her! She was smiling and told me her name... Also, that you would die in a few years when I could take care of myself, on May 5th, the day of her anniversary!

She said she'd be waiting for you in heaven—...

Vincent felt a chill and chose not to continue with the conversation. Jacob communicated with the swallows as if they were other children. He played with them and they sang when he approached them. Stretching his arms, the birds perched on them, his shoulders and his head and let him caress them. He seemed to whistle to them things only they understood. When he was thirteen, he knew by heart all Garcia Lorca's verses his father recited and he could whistle them with great skill as well as many others he invented. His melodies were of a beauty beyond humanity. He became the best whistler in the region, his name soon reached a vast territory and people began calling him 'the Swallows Tamer' and look for him, hoping to touch him, or asking him for healing and miracles. They thought a young man with that gift was another Saint Francis or a heavenly messenger, and heard that during the Virgin's apparitions in several places, she's always surrounded by small birds singing with joy. So, unintentionally, Jacob and his father began to amass a small fortune with the money people gave hoping to see a miracle.

Vincent built a wooden box with a slot on top and a brass sign with words inscribed in it where he wrote: 'Hope Box' and stuck it to the wagon's side, where, without asking anything, people voluntarily deposited their petitions and their savings. They came with all kinds of needs: blind, lame, maimed, crippled and deformed, loves lost and loves needing disappear without pain, desires, hopes and frustrations. After some time, the box was filled, Vincent divided its content in two halves. One part was handed to the poorest he found that day on his way and the other he kept it in a bag for times of scarcity.

In a small town's church, he heard a sermon that's

always better to sleep with one's head pointing north and never south. Those who slept with their heads pointing south were susceptible to infections, sins, crimes and blunders. He also said, one should never build a house on a groundwater's flow and taught that evil could not nest in the hearts of small birds but only in those of owls, crows, vultures and prey birds. From all of these the worst were the owls, chosen by the wizards and sorcerers from ancient times as symbols of the devil. The same priest asked parishioners to avoid short-haired dogs, which could easily fall prey to the spirits of the damned roaming earth. To end spells, he said, the best remedy was to place a honey's bottle under the bed. Bad influences or any spells and incantations would be trapped inside the bottle and the honey would never let them leave. The worst of those spirits were hidden in wooden objects that once served to demonic cults. No one seemed to believe much, because the priest was known to own a book with strange revelations which sometimes quoted and that no one ever heard about, however, the sermon that morning was catastrophic for the poor dogs that roamed the plaza. On leaving the church, some of them were killed or beaten with sticks by frightened parishioners.

Soon the wonders of Jacob's gifts reached the priest's ears. Jealous, due to the decrease in income, suspected that parishioners preferred to give that to a young man who spoke with birds than to a priest who preached hidden revelations with esoteric overtones shouting from the pulpit things that scared them. The punishments from the Book of Revelation were his specialty, but people had tired of hearing them, and though everyone knew they were coming, nobody thought of them anymore.

The priest's response was not delayed. Ordered his secretary, a petty and envious woman who at one time was a banker and sought shelter in his parish on the pretext to help manage his finances, to hire some bullies to beat Jacob and his father and she did.

After midnight, when everyone was asleep, and the moon hid behind clouds, 'Miracles', the bitch that always travelled with them began to bark. In the shadows, like swift ghosts with lit torches in their hands as way of clubs, the big boys jumped from the cliffs on either side of the road and placed themselves beside the cart, ready to beat up the occupants, putting the wagon on fire after. But a great surprise awaited them. Hundreds of large and small birds rushed at them, pecking as they could, with such determination that in the midst of cries and surrounded by the fluttering, fled in terror to the village where they arrived bleeding. When Jacob and his father woke up, went outside the wagon to see what was happening but they couldn't do anything, even though Jacob whistled calling the birds, they ignored him. So, they decided to leave the town that night, before the attackers' relatives, the secretary and the priest took more reprisals. They went to another place looking for new airs across a canyon where a crystalline river flowed jumping between stones, crossed it and they saw from the distance the white lime painted towers of the village's church also lost in the mountains and headed in that direction, but Providence's designs changed their plans in a blow.

It happened that afternoon when Vincent gave the mare a break, releasing it from the harness while he taught his son "The Wrath", his favourite poem by Octavio Paz. Suddenly a storm arose and big drops began to fall. Flashes lit up the landscape and thunders rumbled with echoes as celestial giant drums. When Vincent came to fetch the animal, heard a snap like a whip in the air. A lightning bolt fell on him killing him instantly, turning him into a pile of charred smoking flesh. Jacob had no time to help him. When he saw his father in that state, jumped out of the wagon, he knelt at his side and whistled the *Magnificat* offering his tears for him.

○○○

The hard but happy life on the cart next to Vincent, had taught him to accept things the way they are. Without thinking twice, when the storm subsided, he sought the shovel and began digging a hole beside the road; there buried his last tears and what was left of his beloved father's body; built on top a stone mound, then found two pieces of wood, he built a cross and he placed it in the centre of the tomb and entangled in it her mother's amethyst crystal rosary. Henceforth he should fend for himself. The gifts he was born with would enable his subsistence, or so he thought. Then he remembered Vincent's words putting a hand on his forehead whispering on a dark night:

— *"Jacob, never be discouraged, always merge with the breath you have left! Use your gifts; do whatever makes you happy and if you do not know the answer search for it until you find it. Do not forget, you have a magical name that will allow you to transcend. All you have to do is follow your own instincts and let yourself be guided by the voice of your conscience that is the voice of your soul, the true light of hope in you. No matter what happens, I will always be by your side guiding you in your endeavour. The spirit of your mother is with you also and it will also guide you with love.*
It is easier for her to do so from heaven."

And so, thinking of those words he placed the harness on his mare and decided to move from there, the swallows always with him, accompanying in silence. Soon the night like a stars' blanket covered everything and that was the first time he felt a deep loneliness and fascinating sadness … He hadn't eaten yet, but he wasn't hungry, the last ham and loaf of rye bread that his father managed to redeem in exchange for reciting an entire chapter of *"Don Quixote"* were still intact. Suddenly, a half-moon bite like a piece of stale cheese appeared on the horizon and the stars lost some of their brilliance. Jacob decided to follow whatever path his mare took in the middle of the night. A couple of dusty tears marking his cheeks rolled down his neck.

The wagon began to move. At that moment he heard a different sound than the one made by the animal's hooves when hitting the gravels on the road or than the one produced by the squeak of his cart's springs. It was a pristine noise like that one of crystal cups hitting another. The mare had scarcely moved five paces when a sudden ray of light filtered through the clouds and illuminated the scene. He looked at both sides of the trail hoping to find the source of the sound and saw a cross to the right side and at the centre of it a blue glow. Stopped the wagon, cautiously approached and saw what the ray's light showed; embedded in the cross it was a brass medallion and a date inscribed on it with the words

"Ruth, May 5th".

It was the same day his mother had died fifteen years ago and near the same place where he buried his father. Then he remembered his vision. His father had gone to meet her mother that evening, as predicted.

He slept that night, lying beside the cross wrapped with the memory of a woman he'd never touched but with whom he dreamed of many times, a woman he knew because of what his father told him. That night Vincent and Ruth decided to continue their eternal journey together, leaving their only son alone to experience the thousand colours of life, the butterfly's wings flying in the mountains, the valleys of his native land and the secrets of the constellations that came with the evening when the shadows had sucked the light of day. All had been designed by that invisible and powerful hand, that master-crafted all things since eternity.

At the time, lost in the trails of his homeland, one could still see crosses of all sizes of those who had died because of a futile war that led some to deny their own dead. An archbishop said somewhere that evil's forces had conspired to defeat the good's forces. But tragedies in his country were soon forgotten and memory was short. It was a matter of time before people erased a stroke of tragedy permanently lived, due to those who banished justice out of the land and therefore forgot peace. And this was how things were: indolence took over the hearts of many who now cared for nothing. If the harvest was good, people buried their past with the boom and greed took roots in the hole left by the uprooting of justice.

Many wondered from where that malignant heritage came. Some blamed it on the ancient Indian tribes with their flaws, brutal and bloody ritual customs, eating their enemies' hearts in ceremonies still remembered. Others blamed bad influences on the Arabs who in their eagerness to trade everything permeated with their deceptive practices and gadgets the soul of those who got in contact with them, carrying that bad heredity to the New World. But there were those who blamed blacks and gypsies with their rites brought from the dense Congo's jungles and beyond the Carpathians. Finally, others said the culprit was religion, which led the abhorrent practice of merciless inquisitors in their quest for gold, to rob the Indians of any golden idol they could lay their hands on to melt it on their behalf.

The truth is that all were guilty, but the only, the real culprit was the same old thing that everywhere and at all times was present. The demon of greed, wearing a thousand disguises, using idols, harvest, death, revenge, crosses without names, lust, loneliness, sadness, desolation and despair; the demon of frustration and heartbreak. Yes, he was the real culprit, more than any other; the demon called 'indifference'. But his land was saved by the innocence's angel, because in spite of so much darkness, there were also lurked light's flashes, purity, grace and ease, of endless clouds' horizons, coloured' seas, diaphanous air, mountains, deserts and jungles covering vast territories where an untouched, full, overflowing living nature, could still be experienced.

So, his fate oscillated like a pendulum: at one end was love, and fear in the other. He was In between. The pendulum always swinging from one end to the other, sounding like a heartbeat, which would only shut up with his death. At that point, he hoped, he'd find the true meaning of his life.

Next day he heard a commotion in the distance and the bells of a church calling the faithful to attend. He still kept some of his savings in the 'Hope Box', and thought of giving alms ordering some masses for his parents. A loudspeaker mounted on the roof of a rickety wagon, painted with clowns' figures on the side announcing the circus and the circus gypsies, invited everyone to come. He parked his cart next to a treadmill near the town's square. Stunned by the sounds' pandemonium that followed; he saw from afar the winding bodies of two women with two separate earthen jars on their heads, both moving toward him. They seemed to move their bodies in a synchronized rhythmical slow cadence, like palm trees hit by a gentle breeze. They wore silk's breeches, tinted in crimson and blue shades, veils wrapped around their heads and bodies which moved when they walked. As they approached, Jacob could make their skin the colour of cinnamon and their deep black eyes, bright as the stars of the night before. Both smiled simultaneously showing white perfect teeth like pearls contrasting with their toasted skin's colour.

They seemed happy and sad at the same time; a combination difficult to elucidate. One had long fingers covered with silver rings inscribed with lapis-lazuli and the other arms covered with gold and copper bracelets. Their silhouettes were thin and their naked bellies and hips were moving in harmony with a magic cadence that touched every fibre of his being. Their hard bodies and their breast's nipples were drawn under the silk moved by the wind. The two women were almost identical to the eye. The one on the left put her jug on the floor and spoke with a mischievous look.

—My name is Samira... she is my sister Sahay. We're twins. Want a drink of water or perhaps fruit wine for something to eat? I can read your palm's hands and my sister Sahay the Tarot's cards. Don't be afraid; let me see your palms.

Jacob with some suspicion spread his hands and then whistled.

—I've only one loaf of rye bread and a piece of lamb ham to share—... They looked in wonder, spellbound by his whistle and then Samira asked incredulous.

—Who taught you to whistle like that?

—No one, he hissed. I was born like this. My father said it was a gift, but since yesterday I'm an orphan... he went to heaven to meet my mother. From now on I'll have to cope alone. Now tell me, will you share my food? I'm thirsty and I'd like a drink of water or wine. —Then Sahay said without hesitation:

—Why not? He, who shares his bread shares it all.

Then Samira remained pensive for a moment as she watched Jacob hand's palms. She began to travel the marked lines with the tips of her fingers and stared into his eyes. With every touch Jacob was awakened in his body more and more and the two women, like two cobras stalking its prey, seemed to perceive it. Suddenly Samira gave a surprise's cry and exclaimed filled with emotion, almost in tears:

—I see your destiny it's marked by someone very powerful and your mission will have a strange ending. Something will happen in your life that may soon change your gifts' course... Ah! From the seven types of hands that exist, you've a bit of all! I never saw anything like it! There is a legend in our traditions: he who possesses the characteristics of the seven hands is designed to teach, heal and give everything. I feel a lucky woman to have met you. I'd like your hands to caress my body! Want to know more?

—I have all the time in the world, Jacob hissed. What more can you tell me?

—Well, this is the strangest thing I've seen—, she said in astonishment—. Of the four temperaments that exist, you also possess them all. The lines in your hand denote much more. You could have a long life, but a great love will end its course earlier than expected. You'll have three children, two boys and one girl—. Again, in a voice choked with surprise exclaimed:

—I also see that your future and ours are intertwined forever! Tell me, do you've any woman in your life?

—No—, whistled Jacob.

—Want to join us? Sahay asked with a laugh.

—I'm not sure if I should. I have no experience in these matters...

—Don't worry; you don't have to know or do anything. We'll do everything for you. We can teach you. We've never been with a man like you. Come, let us go inside the wagon and pull down the canvas in the back...

Jacob woke up next morning and didn't know whether he did or dreamed what it actually happened. Stretched his arms, gave a long yawn and when he looked for Samira found her body at his side. She seemed to be asleep with a smile on her face; grabbed her hair in his hands letting it slip through his fingers. Her cinnamon skin showed a wonderful brilliance, and her hands with long fingers covered with rings of silver inlaid with lapis-lazuli shone with the sun's rays filtering through the wagon's canvas.

Felt the urgency to wake her up and kiss her again. At that moment he experienced a change and felt the need to talk. First, gently he called her name and this was the first time he ever heard his own words. He was amazed! Noted he could pronounce them with perfect clarity. Something had happened to him. If it was a blessing or a curse, only time could tell, but the truth is that his life would never be the same. With the loss of innocence something more was added to his process of growth: the human speech. He thought it was a shame his father wasn't there to witness that moment, he turned his head to the other side and found Sahay's back, bright also, resembling golden dunes and desert views from afar. Samira woke up first and said in a sleepy voice:

— I dreamed you were talking... and called me by my name...

—That wasn't a dream... I called you by your name! From this morning I can talk, something happened to me, I feel I'm like any other human being!

—I never imagined you were like this. Last night you made me feel something I've never experienced before—. Then Sahay opened her eyes and turned around saying:

—Yeah, yeah—, she said with a smile, —you've a gift that not only serves to whistle words. Your touch made me different, as a rose that finally opened its petals to the sun. You know how to reach a woman's heart by not asking anything for you. I'll be unconditionally yours for as long as you want me to. You can always have us both if you wish. Tell us, would you like to live with us—? Samira interrupted with enthusiasm…

—With your whistle you could join the circus and perhaps become a member of the tribe, but first we must ask Tlosh, our father, if you can join our 'vurdum' (caravan). Before his eyes you must decide only for one of us, but secretly, we'll both love you and you can do the same. We'll tell him you are a gypsy and walk alone. Your whistle and your birds will open the way. Do you speak or understand our language the Romani?

—I understand every language on earth ... I was born with that gift. But last night I bit the forbidden fruit and I woke up seeing things differently, I learned to speak and express myself as I'd never done before. It is like if I'd broken a sacred bond with my past. Having met you, have changed my life forever.

—What do you know of our laws? —Asked Samira again.

—Nothing, I'll have to learn them.

○○○

During the following days, both twins visited him in secrecy when they could and taught him the laws and ancient Gypsies' traditions, until the time came when both took him into the circus and presented him to their father. As always, Jacob was accompanied by the swallows which followed him everywhere and for the first time he was singing on the road a chorus that went like this:

"And it was that magic night,
I felt something in the wind
getting deep inside of me,
like the power of a sting

or the venom of a bee
I woke up with new cords,
Getting into the world of words,
I received a new light',
deep, deep inside of me…"

Tlosh then decided to test the purity of Jacob's blood. After hearing his whistle and asking many questions, at Samira's suggestion Jacob changed his name to Rish and said he was an orphan come from the country beyond the waters—. Tlosh saw in his daughter's face her passion for him and decided to measure his future son in law. The test would be terrible. Yabor, the former Samira's fiancé would challenge him to a knives duel after midnight in the circus' arena. If he emerged victorious would be considered a sure sign, if either of them died, his corpse would be buried beside the road with nothing to indicate who was there.

At midnight there was a dance invoking the spirit of the night, the angel of death. Four fires marking the cardinal points went on in the arena and sounds of drums, cymbals and flutes began to mingle in that coven come from distant times, when a man learned to live with fire. The wail of an old violin, ripped through the night's air, while the violinist's fingers moved like agile spiders across the strings, with each note escaping the bow's chase. When the violinist took out the last note of his tool, the twins that remained very still began a fast dance moving their hips in frenzy, with their bare bellies shining with sweat, falling finally to the ground remaining there, motionless, like two dead pigeons. The two opponents with naked torsos were placed face to face within walking distance one from the other. Jacob had never fought another man. Yabor raised his right hand and pointing him with a hoarse voice spit a gypsy curse as if coming from the bowels of hell.

—'*Amria*'—! Yabor shouted with all his might. —

'Gadje'! -No Gypsy! -

Samira shouted angrily:

—*'Arakav Tut'! -Be careful! -*

Jacob dropped his knife on the sand and whistled. Four hawks standing on the bar used by acrobats swooped down with shrill cries and rushed on Yabor. He yelled in panic:

—*He is possessed by 'Kesali'! -The spirit of the woods-. He's an 'O Beng'! –Demon-.*

Then he ran terrified while being chased by the birds, falling over a cliff, exhausted, senseless, with a bleeding body, marked by bruises. Jacob went after him. When he found him, he lifts him up, and took him back under the tent, holding his lacerated body with compassion and carefully placed him on the sand. Then, Tlosh said: — "Drava… Baxt… Ashen Devlesa!" -You've the real gypsies' magic... Good luck... God be with you! -

This gesture won him the sympathy of his new tribe. He wasn't an orphan anymore. In the midst of sounds, smells of perfumes and ancestral incenses the welcoming party lasted until dawn. From that night on, the upcoming Samira's wedding was secretly kept in Tlosh' mind; it would take place several weeks later. As days passed by, he taught Jacob to tame horses with a gypsy secret, an art that made them docile when riding, but with a nasty mania: the horses stopped at once to see a bird, throwing over its heads its unsuspecting riders. Then the owners came back again and offered a quarter of the price they paid for them, so the gypsies sold and resold their horses again and again.

Soon, Jacob's fame became legendary and reached the ears of a music teacher and a linguist who both agreed to visit him. After hearing Jacob were astonished by his gifts and upon their return spread the news back in the city. A university rector, when read about it, decided to visit him too and made him an offer. When he got to the gypsy camp, Tlosh intercepted him and requested a great amount of money on condition that someday he'd recover his future son in law. And so, Jacob was sold like a horse, Tlosh in the hope that his attraction to Samira would return him to the tribe one day, but it didn't. Time passed and he never came back. The gypsy curse that Yabor uttered was met. Samira never married, becoming sad, burdened with nostalgia. She seemed always wrapped in a deep loneliness and fascinating sadness, until one day she left the caravan, and in spite of everyone looking and asking for her whereabouts, no one saw her again, as if disappearing by magic from the face of the earth. Fear came upon all, but no one ever imagined the outcome destiny had prepared for her and what the future would bring. In the meantime, Jacob's prestige went through the roof. Soon he forgot about the gypsies, his world changed with the continuing turning of the spiral that shaped the swirl of his life.

When he reached the big city, he rented an apartment next door to the university where he taught, he was the youngest professor in that school and hardly had outgrown puberty. His youth brought him new friends and of course, was quick to meet a woman. Her name was Simona; they were almost the same age; he met her one afternoon in the library, she was very beautiful and shapely as a mature fruit. Her hair and eyes were shiny black and she had a smile that seemed a pearl necklace. He marvelled at her face the first time he saw her. She studied history and then he took the same classes she did so they could see each other more often. He also took the occasion to expand his knowledge in all areas that interested him.

At the age of twenty he became a man of letters, at twenty-two he graduated as a philosopher, at twenty-four he became an ecologist, an anthropologist at twenty-six, at twenty-eight a geologist, an astronomer at twenty-nine, at thirty-one he graduated in astrophysics, and by that time Simona was his wife and had two children with her. Over time, Simona disappeared from his life and fled with an editor in search of fortune, taking their children with her, but was never happy. The editor was unfaithful whenever he could and when she wanted to return, she suffered an amoebae's attack to the liver and died shortly after. Following the angels' command, he continued writing. His memories began to flow as he wrote. At a moment he felt afraid, a strange force reminded him of Tania, the woman who spoke in such a high pitch that sometimes broke the glasses. That was perhaps one of the bitterest periods of his life, changing his faith for a false idol who thought he could love, but in time cost him what remained of his laughter and the ability to be himself.

The day he met her at a flea's market, he didn't suspect that Yabor, had sent her loaded with spells to end his life. She read for him the bottom of a chocolate's cup and the tarot's cards and she saw in him something of a genius and a saint, of a devil and a child. She predicted he'd be famous and a great love would lead him to his grave. Her yellow eyes were fixed on him with the intensity of a snake stalking at its prey. He forgot what happened afterwards…

Time passed and he observed that a man of short stature and a large brimmed hat followed him everywhere he went either in the park or out of the university where he taught. But one day, Dalila, one of his students who kept a secret love for him, noticed it too and made him a warning:

—Jacob, be careful! I saw a man following you. I suspect he is a wizard, a gypsy or an incubus. He wears a big hat, but that's only part of his disguise. After some time to secretly observe his movements, a couple of days ago I followed him to a nearby stretch in the mountain arriving to a well formed by the ravine near the village. He tried to seduce a beautiful woman bathing in the well. She, as a precaution remained submerged to the neck. As murderers, thieves, sorcerers and incubi are afraid of clean water, he waited for a long time for her to come out, seeing that she didn't, he flew into a rage and marched through the forest singing and playing a flute, wrapped in a catchy melody that soon invaded every corner of the woods. His pace had something come from another world and sang like this:

"My music will make you my instrument,
And its rhythm will give me your mind.

My music will make you my instrument,
And its rhythm will give me your mind."

He crossed back the plaza with me and I began follow him again, this time the woman was combing her hair near the banks of the same well when she heard a song coming from the woods, being delighted by the rhythm. Suddenly, the small man left the forest and she recognized him but this time failed to stop his advances. The strange melody put her into a hypnotic state similar to a deep sleep, when she awoke, she felt different, becoming another Tania. The women possessed by sorcerers and incubi are called succubus and only follow orders from those who seduced them with their spells and incantations.

—It's terrible! —Answered him with fright, thanks for warning me, is there really any way to release them from the spell?

— It's very difficult—, said Dalila. —The best thing, as I read, is to find a holy man with special powers to help you, otherwise you might fall under evil's control losing all hope. Succubus were camouflaged from ancient times resembling the stones supporting the roofs and domes of old gothic cathedrals. Others are stone gargoyles that spit water when it rains. In both cases seem to be tied to the stone, watching from above to anyone who enters the premises, but don't be fooled, they're just there waiting for whoever comes to conjure them. On some occasions, men who seduce women use amulets and magic to retain them and the same happens the other way around… it's simply part of human nature, when that occurs, only a holy man can undo the evil bond.

But nothing helped the warning. During the time he was under Tania' spell, his children didn't know where he was and no one came to know of his existence. She fed only on dry grain and so it was her heart. In the meantime, Jacob's whereabouts reached all earth's corners. Everyone asked where he was hiding. Newspapers wrote news speculating about his disappearance. Some said he was in a convent, protected by Tibetan monks, others guessed he found an ice age's cave and hid in there, fleeing human vanity, but still others proclaimed his death as a result of an accident or a kidnapping.

On the doorstep of a church many faithful people organized a vigil in his honour. Thousands of candles were placed at the atrium's entrance for thirty-three days as a way of exorcism. Cards and flowers from all over the world called for his body's return and the true story of what happened. There were so many offerings that it became impossible to enter the church, blocking entrances to above its doors. As days passed, the court was cleared and people began to forget about him, however, a bronze statue was donated anonymously by a convent. In it he appeared with his arms covered with birds, and an inscription engraved on its base:

"Here is Jacob
the one born to heal the heart
who spoke all languages of men
who inspired goodness where he went

and with the single touch of hands,
understood the humans with his art."

When he met Tania lost all his gifts in an instant. The gift of tears served him to confirm the most important decisions of his life easing his mind of guilt's weight. Tears came to him freely without request, sometimes when meditating or practicing charity and others when whistling or writing. Tania stole his heart and locked it in a hard shell as if hidden in a nut. Never again, laughed or whistled while he was at her side. He was tied ever since with a heavy chain around his neck impossible to break. His feelings were frozen like in a stone tower, and entered the world of the expressionless dead. Only Vincent's or the gypsies' memories were all that animated his hope. Eventually his eyes lost all brilliance and expression. Tania never loved him, just waited to grab his conscience and property, including his own life.

She seemed crazy or possessed by three spirits he had identified, one was the spirit of anger that forced her to commit acts of which later could not remember, other was a mocking and irreverent one with all the important and sacred, and the third was a sad one stealing any moment of happiness when he was around. She meditated three times a day and used to invoke 'mantras' with Tibetan demons' names with a hoarse voice as coming from the depths of hell filling him with horror. He could never bear the sweet smell of burning incenses that filled the house, attracting flies by the sticky perfume or who knows by what other reason. One Sunday, while attending to Mass, Tania went to the flea's market that took place in the square opposite the church. That morning Jacob's prayers were answered and managed to break the spell. When the ceremony ended, he stood on the atrium and saw Tania from afar talking to Yabor, who must have thought that the curse that bound his old rival to the gypsy succubus had been his best revenge. But in an instant thing changed. He saw when he bought six incense sticks, six dried flowers and six amulets and hung them to her neck, then both took off their sandals and embraced each other, departing together for never return. Tania that day went with someone like her, who henceforth could share the same sweetish smell of incenses and the flavour of dried nuts. That morning the curse changed hands.

When he saw them leaving, he felt the heavy chain that bound him removed and his life was his again. Still unaccustomed to his new self, he felt very light, as if he weighed nothing and looked down at his feet to see if they rested on the ground. At the corner of the square he saw the children's hospice playing with a colour ball and two blackbirds who disputed a piece of bread on the sidewalk. He called them with a whistle and they obeyed resting on his shoulders. He had recovered his gift. On the corner, the smell of freshly roasted caramel apples sprinkled with butter and cinnamon powder mixed with the smoke of the coals. The seller of cotton candy strung on bamboo splinters forming a pink tree, called the people to buy one and a puppeteer down the plaza presented his only show: *"The triumph of comedy over tragedy."* This involved using two puppets he operated with his fingers, each hidden behind a white mask; one represented laughter and other pain. Why always won *"the comedy"* he never understood. In the centre of the square, two old men sat down to discuss something sharing a bag of popcorn with salt and dozens of pigeons swarmed around them, waiting for the leftovers. The newspapers' seller announcing the news and a literary supplement was also there. He considered himself a patriot, so he was excited when he saw the tricolour flags' vendor wandering around the square. In the shade of a pine tree behind her easel, was Agnes, who painted sunflowers and fruit floating on the sea. He admired her surrealistic art, in the past they talked often and discover that they had the same taste for music, both loved Beethoven's, barley soup or lentils with hot chili. This time Agnes painted a sea horse floating on the cloister's roofs. The brown mop dog accompanying the sweet old lady selling milk he didn't see. He went to ask her where it was and she told him it died of old age. Then he realized he spent a time of which he bore no memory. Along the way, tried to put together the puzzle of his lost life, seeing with deep sorrow the traces left its mark. He didn't have the consistency of years before. That afternoon looked at him in the mirror and he didn't like what he saw. His weight had dropped to less than half. His bright eyes of another age were now opaque, lost in its sockets, his brain was tired and his gait was wobbly and uncertain.

The next day he made a decision. With the last breath he'd left, he went to visit the mysterious monk who lived in the dark cloister facing the plaza and had the gift of speaking with the stones. He asked him for help; his life hung by a thread, it was essential somehow to be himself again and he decided to recover using a steel will no matter the sacrifice. Miel watched him as he healed his memories; he still had a long way to go. His frustration was not having listened to the cries of his soul when he was called to be like the monk. He felt jealous of the hermits enclosed in dark caves, away from the world, where only their minds could touch them.

The monk turned out to be the friend he expected. As a young man felt the desire to enter a seminary, but the appearance of Rose dispelled every sign of vocation. Rose loved painters' books. One day she bought one showing the image of a saint in ecstasy at the entrance of a cave, she wrapped it in tissue paper, and sent it with a card and a kiss of the soul. From that day he never saw her again. The monk like the saint ended up living in a cave. When he left, nobody knew where he was. For three years he fed with acorns on full moon nights and allowed himself to grow a long black beard. When he saw the sunshine after so long, pale, gaunt, haggard but rich in spirit and fulfilled with God, he knew his mission was clear. In his abandonment he acquired gifts that no one suspected he had. He realized he was reborn and the mission he'd have to accomplish.

Since then, the monk grew in strength and holiness every day and his gifts began to be legendary. He healed people by laying his hands on them, he could know the past of anyone who passed by in front of him and he had the rare gift of bilocation that allowed him to be in two places at the same time.

When the monk came across the face and emaciated body of his friend after his affair with Tania, he felt deep compassion for him; he realized that he was near to death and his life hung from a thread. Then he called Soledad, the cloister's housekeeper and asked her to aid him. Soledad prepared the clerk's room which was not used since the day he's found naked and embraced as a spider to the cook. It was just as well, times were tough; people gave less alms and couldn't afford to pay anyone to play the bells. Over the following weeks, Soledad devoted to care and feed Jacob as if he were her child. He ate breakfast at noon with a half dozen raw eggs, a quart of malt, and slept the rest of the afternoon. He soon began to gain weight, his eyes shone again; his walk was safe and ended up sleeping eight hours. It was then when he returned home and continued his existence. He began to weave his life as a wicker basket. Every day added something to it which made him grow a little more.

Soon, a small part of himself came back again. He got a big room, not far from the cloister and there he kept a few scraps of paper with memories inherited from his past. Some of his books also were with him and those he had no room to stack in his place he gave them to the hospice's library. He was seen often with his children, and soon was surrounded by the warmth of old students and friends, the swallows and the paddles that moved the boat of his destiny returned as well. Soon the press got wind of his return and all celebrated with joy. The news said he retreated to a monastery to meditate in order to be purified. People loved the ascetics and thought he was one of them. His fame grew again making him someone with an air of being a Tibetan holy man.

His legendary wisdom began regaining new momentum, recalling the attention of many scholars. His fame reached the ears of a famous polyglot who included him in a book of merits. From there, he went to the inventory of the most famous. He began to lecture on many subjects, as birds taught him secrets that nobody knew. Its whistles were recorded by a record company and when they were heard by writers and poets, they cried out for the sounds to be guarded and listed as one of the most important humanity's heritages, coming from the prehistoric times of Atlantis, when their people gathered in palaces, dressed in fantastic silk blue costumes and sang their glories, giving rise to the legend. A time when giants roamed the land, which was filled with evil and all the cleaning of their spells was the song of the poets and the whistling of birds. But one day the poets and birds disappeared, bringing the deluge and everything had to start over from a blot.

Soon he was invited to chair a major symposium. Without any pretensions, he prepared himself to keep the appointed destiny. That night, in dreams, he heard Miel's voice that seemed to come from afar:

—You should write about the symposium. People who read your words will remember your proposals. Unbelievers will see everything in a different way. Believers will have more light and fools they will think twice before denying life. There are many who don't appreciate this gift. Remember, ingratitude is a sin comparable to hypocrisy. Those who fall into this sin will not come to see the reason for their existence and in consequence they will not see a happy destiny.

When he reached the country where the event should take place, its president, accompanied by his ministers, came to meet him. He was greeted with military honours, but to him none of this mattered. First, he whistled the national anthem of his country and then one by one of the host countries. The television networks around the world broadcasted the news. The program was expected to last a couple of days and conferences were aimed at the highest level. Geographers, polyglots, historians, theologians, poets, writers, philosophers, anthropologists and archaeologists had gathered there to hear his teachings. The introduction was made whistling Paulo and Francesca's sin narrated in Dante's Divine Comedy. People applauded wildly for several minutes, but then, the conference focused on heaven's nine circles, which very few knew, since that book only mentioned the nine circles of hell. All had been taught to him by the birds. They had ancient traditions and older memory than that of men.

A huge, golden eagle, shining in the sun, flying very high, visited the highest circles, where winged beings almost transparent lived and they could see in all directions. The eagle told him that from there the world could be seen differently, as it really was. The battle between the forces of good and evil was still going on and from that height many tracks could be seen. The faces of the fallen angels were carved on every continent, at the edges of its shores, on rocks, in the profiles of the mountains and on the sea floor. Some had been carved into deserts and steppes or on the same ice at the poles, in an era in which countries hate or the lines that divide them, didn't exist.

A huge skull with no teeth, the size of a cathedral, was half buried in the middle of desert sand, bearing witness with its sinister smile of the struggle that once took place, when many were killed by other angels and sentenced to remain on earth until Judgment Day.

He spoke of an evil woman sitting on a huge ice throne which could be seen from above and was waiting for the sun to melt her and flood all coasts and punish thus the folly of men. Suddenly a man wearing a white robe and a golden turban interrupted and asked Jacob to explain how the Sahara Desert was in ancient times. He then explained that from the air, the eagle's eyes could discern several things depending on the height and the time things were observed. From the highest point one could glimpse the bones of a huge sea serpent that stretched from Egypt to the Atlantic. Then a theologian, amazed, could not believe what he heard and without a second thought, he asked where he obtained so much knowledge.

—All the information I got comes from the birds—, said calmly. —They know more than us, and their flesh was not corrupted like ours with sins that we have not yet succeeded in banishing. Today's man is nourished by the waste left by the lack of love. We are like hungry vultures, the repositories of thousands of years of shame, revenge and attacks on our planet. Soon we'll reap the consequences. The age of Earth as we know it is ending. I'd like to whistle now Earth's anthem. It's composed in honour of the angels and golden eagles flying in the highs. The refrains are the swallows' chorus.

—How many choruses of birds are there? Asked again the theologian filled with insatiable curiosity.

—Nine, each living in one of the circles of heaven accompanying the angels. The only ones excluded are owls, crows, vultures and birds of prey. The time has come for man to look at himself with his own eye and to decide whether he would live or die. An ancient symbol called the Symbol of the Shū predicted catastrophes since immemorial time. One day the emperor of a country came to invite all mankind to decipher it and nobody could

do it, but the birds were able to reveal the secret. Then they told the secret to a poet, the poet to a philosopher and the philosopher to a shepherd boy and each wrote one verse thus composing the Earth's Hymn.
The birds' chorus went like this.

"Oh, blessed and ancient land
who gently caressed us with your hand,
with the tenderness of a loving woman
hoping to find her man,
you gave us the best inside of you
hidden in the Symbol of the Shū."

Then the poet recited:

"Oh, deep and immense sea
filled with moving waves
you were prepared
and when the Flood arrived
didn't take you by surprise.
Oh, quiet and calm waters of blue lakes
the flood made you disappear
and without notice
drowned every human being
sending thunders and strokes."

After that the philosopher spoke:

"Oh, Earth ignored, neglected,
forgotten, lost and outraged
the time has come

for you to take revenge
with a whip, opening
new wounds in the skin
leaving the flesh exposed
in pain without remorse
without forgiveness,
without love."

Then the shepherd boy sung:

"Oh, dear and perfumed earth,
you gave us life and rain,
mountains, seas and deserts.
Be patient with all of humanity
which is desperate
carrying heavy chains
look at us with pity
oh dear mother
give us one more chance
to heal your wounds
and ease the pains."

Finally, Jacob whistled:

"Oh, Earth that gave me love,
take now everything from me,
teach me not to get but to give,
to be united in this path
Oh dreamland, beloved, fragrant,
the time to follow you has come
once you leave behind your wrath."

When the cheering stopped that day, a man in the crowed hiding under a wide-brimmed showing his red hair escaping in disorder beneath it, asked sarcastically:

—What can you tell us about the chest containing the secrets of life's origins? I'm in its search, is part of my destiny.

—Well it's also part of mine.

—The first one to find it will have an immense power. You think you're the best person for this job?

—Yes, he replied in a calm voice, —I'm not interested in power. When I find it, I'll be prepared to give myself and the chest to every human being who needs us.

—Well, I am interested; if I can find it first, you'll know I've it. I bet your soul on mine that I'll find it first…

—I don't make bets. On the other hand, my soul is all that counts and it is not for play or sale, the rest is accessory. Without the soul one can't have the mystical experience of the other dimension.

—In other words, are you saying that science and religion are the same thing? History shows us that they've excluded each other.

—Some people have not understood the true meaning of science and others of religion. Let me explain. There is a Commandment that says: 'Thou shalt not kill'. When I point a telescope at a distant world, I can't see any mosquitoes, but in the end, that's the most important thing I want to find. A small sign of life elsewhere in the cosmos and then you wonder. Would I kill that mosquito if I find it? … Or just let it be alive. I'm sure most of these chorus would beg me to let it live and here is where religion, science and the commandment *"Thou shalt not kill"* converge and takes on great significance. I ask you again. So far, I've considered killing a mosquito … but, what do you think when it comes to killing a man? Some people are not satisfied with destroying one and seek to annihilate millions.

Then the man with wide brim hat frowned and left the auditorium with blazing eyes. On the symposium's third day results were summarized in a proposal. Before leaving, the representatives of all nations signed an agreement that, coinciding with seasons' change, four feasts should be held in Earth's honour.

The first should be: The Feast of Silence. Loudspeakers and all engines should be shut down to avoid altering the course of birds and creatures inhabiting the seas.

The second: The Feast of Night. Cities should remain in the dark, to give a break to Earth, benefiting all beings that longed to return to see the glow of more distant stars or were guided by them, helping cool the planet. Such was the pollution produced by light, which from the air the surface seemed to be on fire or after an explosion.

The third: The Feast of Air and Water. All vehicles should stop, everybody should plant trees, suspend the destruction of forests and save the water, stopping for a short period of time the destruction of the ozone layer, stopping the drought.

The fourth: The Feast of Living Things. Killings of men, whales, sharks, birds, cattle and other animals living on land, air or sea should be suspended for one day.

Scientists agreed to found Earth's University, based in a country that had never seen war. Then they searched for it but didn't find it. At Jacob's suggestion they decided to build a platform in no one waters with a 'permanent council for the environment' consisting of those, always ready to improve the planet and the consciousness of men. An award it was created with the Order of the Grand Toucan to honour the most responsible with creative solutions to save the planet. But greed would take hold in the hearts and minds of rulers and when they decided to implement with new measures these ideas, then, it would prove too late. Earth would change forever and no longer be the same.

Upon his return, remembering all this, he realized that his destiny always formed part of a puzzle designed by a mighty hand. But still he didn't understand what was expected of him. Why Miel appeared, it was not clear. He thought of Crystal, his last love, and then took an inventory of all the moments spent with her and wondered what it would have to do with his fate. The night was cold and the sun still roamed the sky without showing up on the horizon. With effort he came to the fireplace, light it and managed to warm up his hands and feet. The flames brought her face. He thought of calling her to tell her what happened, but he'd not wake her up. He'd talk to her during the day, again he took his notebook in his hand, opened it and read the words blurred with his tears. That night, a still owl watched him from it nest in the oak tree. Unseen, from the other end of the room, the angel Miel also watched. Jacob felt the presence of good and evil. A chill ran down his spine. His adventure was just beginning.

II

With the first rays of the sun, Jacob continued writing about the memory of his encounter with the angel Miel, but he didn't know for sure if he'd dreamed it all. Everything was too real and the bittersweet pain was still burning in the middle of his chest. He touched his belly again looking for his entrails, he was not sure if they were still there. He took back the pen with trembling fingers but again the tears fell sometimes on the white sheets of the scrawl notebook as tiny magnifiers, diluting the ink and scribbles that only he could understand. For years he wrote at least one page each day, as a discipline to relieve his mind so he could sleep in moments of wakefulness. His prayers, sins, obligations, pains, debt, grudges, fears, expectations and the words he wanted to tell to Crystal, the love of his life. He immersed himself in the memories of the woman he loved and returned to live every moment of her past with her. The memories came like lightning coming from the depths of his mind and began to take shape. Weariness finally overcame him again, his head leaned against his chest, and his pen fell from his hand staining the floor with ink, like a wounded bird blood's drops and the memories started to become dreams.

When he came into her life, Crystal thought he'd appeared to her as an angel or perhaps the devil himself. She wasn't sure to love again and if that happened this time would come with her partner to the altar. She wanted to marry and to be sure that nothing and no one could steal one bit of her happiness. She dreamed of having children and a house full of laughter and murmurs. Then he remembered the voices in the elevator when they met and each realized the presence of the other. It was crowded, but the scent of roses emanating from her skin outshone the rest. All were going to the same floor like bees to a hive, being attentive at the stop on the 16th floor. When the door opened, all trooped out to line up against the window of the government pension fund. Only they didn't, and spoke for the first time. She had perceived the fragrance of his cologne, he the beauty of her face, and then asked with a sincere interest.

—What is your name?

—Crystal.

—You've a name the colour of your eyes and eyes the colour of your name, full of stars, she smiled and answered.

—My eyes, or my name?

—Both are so clean, like a landscape of crystal-clear sea or the sky at noon.

—I'm blind, she said with a tinge of sadness—. I am guided by flashes of light and shadow. I live in a dream, in a world of memories. When I was fifteen, my father took me to walk down a mountain in order to better see a solar eclipse. I remember an ad with a woman who looked like me and that was the last time I saw. I like your voice; I would like to touch your face to 'see' you. May I? What's your name?

—Jacob...

—Ah! You've a philosopher's name… also of a love, or a stubborn horse like the one I once had with my father—. He laughed…

—How do you know all that?

—I'm intuitive. I also love finger reading and I like to sing. I am a music teacher at Clarita's nuns' school, next to the monk's cloister, the one who has mysterious gifts. Long ago my father told me stories with horses I still remember. I've been an

42

orphan for several years. I love horses since childhood…

—What a coincidence! I know the same monk. I am a philosopher and I'm stubborn, I like horses when they are free and run through the countryside. Once I wrote something about them. I've the poem with me in my notebook, sometimes I take it everywhere with me.

—I wish one day you'd read it to me.

—And I'd like to hear you sing.

—Over a cup of coffee?

—Of course.

Crystal took his arm, they went to the coffee shop and sat down, while he was looking at her eyes, she looked at his soul and talked…

— I'd never seen eyes so blue and so bright—. He said. She thought his voice was like a dance sound and she gave thanks for her blindness, she learned to live with it, watching with her hands and with her spirit, using them as her eyes.

That evening, under the shade of a silver eucalyptus he told her stories of his life with Vincent. His childhood memories again filled him with emotion. She listened with his hands in hers, as two doves filled with hope, caressing them not to escape. His stories, showing that part of the fabric of his being and the chiaroscuro of his soul, as if they were part of a litany scented ritual amid the smell of a thousand incenses. Slowly, he was putting together the puzzle of his past, printed on his memory's film.

As a child he heard his father speaking about the heroic and he learned the value of martyrdom. The first had a relationship to life and the second to eternity. Crystal listened in silence. Then he spoke of the strange gift he was born with and told her that perhaps he'd inherited from his mother, but his father insisted it was due to the name by which he was baptized. Vincent, in his heart sensed that one day his son would give the expected results for which he sowed in him everything he knew in the garden of hope. Crystal then thought of her world of darkness and secrets of the soul and deep inside felt the desire to share with this man things he could only understand as no other had. She stood up, walked a few steps alone and felt the wet grass under her bare feet, the hot afternoon sun caressing her face and her hands' palms; she stretched her arms trying to catch the last rays of the sun still licking her body.

That night, in the attic where Crystal lived, she asked him to talk about music. Then they made love until sunrise the thud of raindrops against the window pane, imprisoning within each frame a story, as in a cosmic chess or hopscotch of distant constellations. Suddenly she began to sing. He immersing himself in the mirror as if it were a pond heard the jingle of a stream and the roar of a river falling into the void, crashing in the background like a cataract. Amid the kisses they fell asleep in a long embrace, long as the wall across the street. Back memories crowded in his mind like ghosts trying to escape. One by one the memories paraded like the wagons of a long cargo train: the trips they made, stories, adventures, moments shared with the orphans and the most vulnerable, all wrapped in the magic of a tropic filled with strange contrasts, part of their blood

The river was the first wagon of his memory... Over time he became her eyes. One day he decided to take her to meet the sea. Cartagena with the old walls was her childhood's dream. They embarked and descended the river in a barge powered by a paddle wheel that reminded him the sound produced by the wings of birds. Odours and screams filled the air, children, and fishermen, women selling catfish with fried plantains, cassava, mangoes, tangerines, bananas, coffee and bottled water. Someone offered them a stuffed alligator and a tricolour flag. That land was bountiful, and he loved it with his entrails. He described the river as a still anaconda the colour of mud, lying in the sun. That afternoon, Jacob described the green banks on the sides of the barge and both felt a world of hot and humid perfumes of the earth brought by the wind sweeping over the cover of the barge. The red sunset sun hid behind tall grass, outlining the black horns of two lost cows. Night came with the sounds of thousands of insects and monkeys' cries swinging from the hanging vines from a giant tree. She slept on a cot of cloth and beside her, him in a hammock where mosquitoes would sneak.

They were awakened at midnight with the sweet smell of rum and the moans of a woman about to give birth. The midwife, who was traveling with her, prepared a dish of water from the river and an old towel. The moans of the woman soon became a piercing scream and then they heard the new born crying in the darkness. Then a thud, when the midwife cut the placenta with a machete. Jacob remembered what his father told him of his own birth. They felt connected to life with the strength of a wild untamed tropic. The trip would last a few days before reaching its destination. Everything depended on rainfall and river flow. Further down, the barge ran aground on a sandbar and the midday heat became unbearable. Mosquitoes began to devour them. She seemed not to mind, being always calm. The blacks, mulattos and mestizos discover her goodness and her blindness, they took her like one of their own. They offered their food and rubbed them with rum sharing everything they had and the woman who'd given birth, calmed her son with Crystal's' songs and Jacob's whistling.

And so, days went by while they were looking for the shade of the awning, or sometimes the sun until their skins took the colour of the amber. In those long hours on the river, flocks of parrots and macaws were always accompanying them and placed themselves on the slab, in such amounts that it became impossible to move from side to side. Jacob asked the occupants not to be alarmed; he explained the birds always accompanied him. Crystal thanked life and he felt proud and thankful for her. He watched her and described to her all the moments of light and shade and a ten-foot alligator that was on the shore. It was only a few hours before they reached the port. A salty smell quickly wrapped it all. The wooden houses on stilts were grouped in any manner, as dice at random on a table, in the dark water of the swamp. A shad fisherman greeted showing a huge catch on his raft, its body showed bright silver sparkles in the sun like a giant treasure. Miel whipping him up with memories still seemed to be in a hurry, but the devil was also lurking and would make their path more difficult.

They reached the walls at night, after traveling a stretch, in a wagon with broken shock absorbers, welded to the chassis, in a crazy dance jumps and baskets moved by the wind. Politicians preferred that the road between the sea and the stretch of land that separated the swamp, the devil take it, while they spent the budget of the municipality in beauty pageants. Poor Cartagena would never be the same. It went from being taken for its courage in battle, where people suffered from hunger and cruelty of the pirates or the Inquisition to be the home of corrupt politicians, queens' plate and price speculators. But despite its detractors, many of its charms still remained. The smell of fish, oranges, corn-meat cakes and hot coffee from the port, across the Clock Gate returned their breath. They went to the wall by a ramp adjacent to the market area and sat down to listen. Then she asked him after a long sigh:

—Do you hear it? It's alive, it's its heart. Far away, distant lightning lit up the waves and foam tapes and the smell of salt filled their lungs. A group of gulls and two pelicans, fought for the head of a cod abandoned and half buried in the beach's dark sand. On their return, lanterns of Portal of Santo Domingo, put glitter shimmering on the pink walls and the coffers of a neighbouring balcony to the cloister. Still locked within its walls painted with watercolour tones, the chants of the monks could be heard. A hungry dog stopped to drink from a puddle of urine, its wastewater to the reflection of the moon broke into pieces and a strong breeze swept the streets like a battalion of spirits in search for lonely souls. That night, the air continued to heal the memories of the past. The open window let them get away with the sound of the waves.

He awoke with Crystal's body next to his, the cries of vendors of egg corn cakes with salt, warm black coffee from the corner and the radio blaring music coming from somewhere. Puddles of water on the street had dried in the sun and the dawn breeze as the latest sores of a leper. Under the arcades of the square were the shoe shiners, lottery and coconut vendors making their own chicken pen noise. On the way to the convent on the top of a hill, he saw something that shook him and his hands trembled.

—What do you see? She asked.

—A tree...

He had a moment's hesitation to tell her what he saw, he didn't want to tarnish her memories, but that was life, the good, bad, white, black and grey.

—Only one tree?

—Yes, a black tree, its leaves are formed by thousands of vultures' feathers that cover it and stand still there waiting... it is the tree of misery and death.

She was silent. It was a premonition. Above, the stone arches of the convent were covered with small colourful bougainvillea flowers framing the landscape of the city and the bay. At dusk, a distant sea was lost in the sky stained with the blood of blacks, pirates and heroes who once lived there. That night they dined under the perfume of orange blossoms and orange trees in the yard of a house in the centre of the walled city. The music of a sleepy guitar encouraged Crystal. She asked the man for his instrument and sang a song to her lover, a song coming from Peru describing him, a song both liked to hear:

"...Knight
Knight of fine appearance, sir
A hat...
A hat under a star..."

Her song sneaked between the thousand flowers of a bougainvillea stained as with the colour of fish gills' and other darker like drops of bull's blood, climbed the high walls of the courtyard to escape the street between the prisms that left the battlements... People passing by wondered where that song was coming from and began piling up the gate of the house. The restaurant didn't fit most people but the owners, happy with the night's success, welcomed Crystal and Jacob to share their secrets: Golden crab with garlic in olive oil, snails and clams in red sauce sparkled with sesame. The smell of sauces and fried garlic cooking in clay pots came in with the breeze and began to devour their entrails. Crystal ordered a tamarind juice and he one of 'corozo' with two drops of lemon and remembered her grandmother when she said: *"Remember, all is well when fixed with a lemon!"* For dessert she ordered a bouffant 'passion fruit' in caramel sauce and he, islands floating in custard, topped with plum sauce and a touch of rum. With the aroma of Turkish coffee stuck to the palate they said *"goodnight"*, leaving the song still climbing the courtyard walls painted with a hundred layers of varnish and oxidized white droppings of pigeons that was splashed over the centuries. They walked slowly, following the contours of the wall, like a snake waiting to devour them in the blackness of the night. Turning a corner where hung an old lantern, Crystal's face and body lit with yellow light. The outlines of her figure as taken from an ancient scroll, the shadows on her skin stained with traces of charcoal and ochre sanguine gave the appearance of a tattoo.

Suddenly, while walking along the wall holding hands, he saw a white shadow windswept preventing the passage. She held her breath and stopped. She felt the increased beating of his heart. The spot remained stationary cutting its silhouette against the dim light that reflected what was left of the moon. She felt his fear and a presence, but she could not discern who or what it was before them. Then she asked quietly.

—What do you see? I feel a strong presence near us but I can't discern what it is. However, I feel the sadness and the smell of death...

—There are two whitish shadows, one higher than the other, showing his hands as dry branches felled by the wind... The highest appears to have no head and be ready to block our path. — Then loudly rebuked:

—Who are you? What do you want?

They heard a hoarse voice echoing the sea coming when he spoke.

—I am one whose fate was truncated.

—Explain!

—I died in a battle over two centuries ago. My wife was raped and murdered by pirates in this same spot. Despite her pleas I could not defend her. The rogue, adding to the outrageous crime immediately pounced on me and cut my head of one blow, throwing my body's trunk on my wife. We purge the sin of not having been able to forgive them. Help us...!

—What can we do? He Asked moved.

—Find my head and bodies. Some kind of soul buried them next to the ramp that leads to the wall. We need to forgive those who perpetrated the crime, but we cannot do so if the bones don't appear... Since then we roam through this area where no one dares come after dark.

—What is your name?

—My name is Martin but that it doesn't matter. Everyone knows me as the Cabrero's Ghost. My wife's name is Lupe.

—What do we do once we discover the bones?

—Ordain a mass prayed for her soul... and one prayed for mine; otherwise we will always be attached to this wall. Many years ago, a young man met us and I made him a proposal. He was very poor and when I told him the disgrace of what happened, he offered to order two Masses for our intentions; in return, I promised to make him famous. Having no money, he wrote the story of his encounter with me and sent it anonymously to a local newspaper called *"La Patria"*, which was about to close because of the small crowd it attracted. The next day the story was published on the front page and the newsboys shouted the appearance of a ghost on the walls of the Cabrero's area. The newspaper was sold that day as never before. The story was so successful that the owner was forced to make two extra editions and find the hero of the game, posting several messages asking him to come over to tell new stories and offer him a position in the newspaper. The young man finally showed up and started writing about these meetings we had. We told him many things that happened in those days when I was alive. Being chief guard and protector of the city, I witnessed many things, including the slaughter of innocent nuns and children held in the cloister neighbouring the wall, when an English pirate elevated to the rank of 'Lord of Admiralty' for his shameless king, bombed the city, but he failed in his intent and his losses amounted to 7,000 men. This time the walls resisted the attack and the people had to eat rats, dogs and human flesh to avoid starvation. The despair due to lack of food forced the inhabitants to fry in oil the leather boots and horses' chairs to be able to feed themselves. In the following days, the poor man rose to managing editor and eventually became famous in many other areas. I waited patiently while they fulfilled their part of the covenant with me, but success made him forget. One day he died, leaving his children orphans, while my wife and I continued here, waiting for someone to have mercy for us.

—Ah! Poor man! He shouldn't forget his promises! Many men break their promises and then they have to pay the consequences! What did you do, when pirates haunted the city?

—I organized the defence and turned off many fires. Unfortunately, I didn't have time to take the one at the cloister. Several innocent people died there that day bombed by one of the pirate ships.

—I never heard that story; tell us a little more, if you want. We promise to find your bones, your wife's and a priest to offer two Masses for the intentions that you asked.

—Right, but if you break your promise, remember what happened to the young man when he forgot to fulfil his...

They woke up early with the chiming of bells and decided to go to the offices of the mayor to tell the story. He authorized them to dig where so requested and to his surprise there were the bones of the murdered couple centuries ago. The story soon spread from mouth to mouth like a fire and the ' Cabrero's Ghost ' took shape. At noon they entered the Jesuit church of St. Peter, the sea salt and the smell permeated every wall for centuries, the venue was cool and there would be no more than ten people crying in front of a sarcophagus. As they passed beside the sexton, Jacob paid him to order two masses for the souls of Martin and Lupe fulfilling their part of the covenant so the ghost and his wife could rest in peace.

Once settled he described to Crystal the bones and the

yellow ornament with gold embroidery of a saint buried in a glass case beneath the high altar to protect it from insects and from the hands of the curious. The skull became shiny black with time, it seemed shone with bitumen as a tribute to blacks that the saint during his life baptized. The clerk began to move a censer, the smoke of incense myrrh and frankincense, startled for a moment the demons that haunted the altar from the time of the Inquisition.

The church was white and bear, whitewashed, in the austere style of the Jesuits and the cloister with its dome, reminded the tiara of a pope, looking at the bay. The mortar made from seawater and coral sand, mixed with the blood of slaves who died building it still remained in there... The dome was dyed pink and its ribs like the bones of a skeleton bleached by the sun, returned him to think again about the person for whom the ceremony was being offered that morning. A wooden altar supported by columns with laminated gold leaf, served as background to the altar and lit candles, helped give the impression that to be the gate of heaven in the midst of a fire, proclaiming the glory… that word elusive and unrewarding with those who seek it. Statues of saints' names lost in time were in their niches crowned with golden open shells. The roar of the chorus and the smell of candles carried him to a meeting he didn't expect.

Suddenly he left his body and saw from high above the scene of the funeral. He saw the soul of the dead floating face down on his coffin. It was that of a woman resembling a sheet windswept, taking the body image she had in life and weeping bitterly. People in the church were muttering about the causes of her death. On admission to intensive care her heart stopped beating and in spite of all efforts, the doctors could not revive her. She had five children and she was less than thirty years old.

Jacob looked up and saw the swallows flying around the coffin, they were restless, as if something was about to happen. The funeral ceremony of the deceased was about to end. Their five children surrounding their father while enable to bear their misfortune wept inconsolably. Jacob saw her body from above they were sitting. His spirit moved through the air standing in front of a statue of St. Ignatius wearing her lean black cassock and said with emotion.

—You can help her if you want! Can't you see she has five young children? I'll trade my life for hers if something like that serves you. I've nothing more to offer! At that moment the statue blinked and the saint replied:

—You've said so. I'll be waiting for your time.

Everybody felt a tremor in the church and the coffin lid was opened at once. She sat pale and with a smile she looked upon the present. Everyone was stunned, their jaws unhinged and amid cries of terror, the priest approached her and asked.

—Where are you… in purgatory, heaven or hell?

—I'm on earth—, she replied, I'm back to stay... someone here prayed for me and it was heard. The power of prayer is immense if it's done with the heart!

At that moment Jacob remembered his own miracle, when once, being ten years old, fell off the wagon striking his head against a stone. Vincent took him to the infirmary of a neighbouring town and asked Saint Ignatius not to let his only son die. That night in the dark, surrounded by the smell of disinfectant, the muffled voices of nurses speculated whether he'd live or die. It was Christmas, suddenly he revived! He was alive! His father and the doctor had no doubt of the miracle performed, but Jacob was not entirely convinced. A few days after the accident Vincent took him back to the wagon and spoke with gratitude for the saint.

—I'll nail this picture of St. Ignatius in front of your bed so you'll always remember the one who interceded to save your life. Pray thanking him and always remember him in your prayers.

He wasn't sure if he liked the saint's face; he found him a little harsh, thin, his hooked pointed nose, reminded him the one of his father, his eyes looking a little lost in the past and had something of Don Quixote but the fact is that the stamp was stuck there, like a guardian of his recovery. Next day, the unexpected happened. He opened his eyes and the first thing he saw was not one but two pictures in front of his bed. The saint thus decided to show how powerful his intervention had been. Then he noticed with surprise he was seeing double all the objects inside the wagon. He rang a bell that his father had left him for emergencies and when he came, found him scared with the new events. He immediately took him to the town's ophthalmologist who gave them his opinion: He would not see well at least for a year and suffer severe headaches, and then he dismissed them without giving them any hope in the short term.

That night Jacob spoke to the saint, in a mixture of anger and fear:

—You may think I don't believe in you, and truly I've my doubts, for the miracle of reviving me, you did it to my father. I wonder if you hear me. If that's so, I would like to ask you for a miracle, something in order to believe in you. Give me back my normal vision in four days and then I'll believe. If you do so, I'll pray one Our Father and Hail Mary every day for a whole year in your name, I'll offer communion the first seven holy Fridays also in your name and finally I'll visit your place of birth and pray a Rosary at that site. I know this last part won't be easy but you'll see that I keep my promises.

What he didn't know is that the saint didn't forget them either. Without thinking more fell asleep overcome by tiredness and worry. During the first three days he observed no improvement, the fourth day he woke up at dawn with a strange sense of wellbeing. He opened his eyes and the first thing he did was to look at the picture of the saint, for his surprise he saw only one print. He looked along the other objects in the cart and found that his vision was normal. A deep gratitude and indescribable joy seized him. Then he whistled in excitement.

—I'm cured! I'm cured! I don't see two but one print!

Thereafter, the accident was a thing of the past, the only consequence was the obligation to pay the saint the promise he'd made. Years passed, and he forgot his part of the deal.

With success insured, his fame spread throughout the world and he was invited to give talks in the great peninsula, across the sea. When he completed the cycle for which he was invited, at dawn of the summer, he came whistling down a road the Song of the Earth when he saw below the hill, a village tucked in the mountains, revealing a set of tiled roofs shining with the sun and a river descending jumping between the stones. At that site the road split and flipping a coin in the air he took the deviation on the right and began climbing a mountain. After a while he noticed that the road narrowed following a fairly steep slope amid a forest of pines and complete solitude, where cliffs and precipices forced him to be careful. He glanced at the fuel gauge and realized the tank was almost empty. The sky darkened so that it looked like night and big drops began to fall everywhere, becoming in a few seconds a torrential rain.

Rays to the right and left of the car dazzled him with their light and the deafening roar produced by them when they ripped the air filled him with fear. He could barely see beyond the windshield, he looked at the fuel gauge again and calculated he had barely enough to go for 1 kilometre, so he decided to park after the next turn and wait for someone to pick him up, when the unexpected happened. In the midst of the storm, lightning illuminated a white small ad written in black letters on the right side of the road that said: *"To Loyola 1 kilometre."* He shuddered as he remembered his promise to the saint. Ignatius had been born there and was looking for him!

He came to Loyola almost at night with a damp floor and a freezing cold, once he entered town, the vehicle stopped for lack of fuel exactly in front of the saint's house. He descended of the vehicle and walked to the doors of a small circular basilica marking the place where the saint was baptized. Some Gregorian Chants could be heard nearby. Once he entered the enclosure protected by the shadows, he knelt down and started to pay his promise. He began to pray the Rosary and the Hail Mary piled into his throat. He'd never prayed one before by himself, so he added some prayers to make sure that the saint would not take any retaliation. He recalled with fear that he was somehow vindictive and jealous. When he finished, he heard from above a dry voice that echoed chasing the walls of that room, and looking up he saw amid the shadows an iron railing circling the perimeter. A lean silhouette, dressed with a dark cassock, was limping a bit when walking. Moving behind the railing and leaning on it asked him with a deep hoarsely voice:

—What are you doing here?

He replied invaded by surprise and fear:

—I'm paying a promise…

Then the voice replied:

—Did you do it?

—Yes, I did.

—Then go out and testify!

Suddenly the figure vanished in thin air. He recalled that the saint was lame, receiving a cannon shot in one leg during the Battle of Lepanto. His memories suddenly vanished. His meeting face to face with the saint changed him forever. He thought too many coincidences had occurred that day to indicate that everything was a miracle. Things just didn't happen that way. Miracles were necessary to strengthen faith and faith was necessary to obtain miracles and both, miracles and faith were necessary in any healing process that would last a life time.

That night, before dawn, Miel appeared again, this time wearing a gleaming sword made of fire and his feet were on the ground. When he opened his eyes, he was involved in a blaze, then he spoke in a firm and serene voice:

—I know how much you loved her, but now you need to see more. I promised to visit you and tell you about the story of the Big Tree. There is a very old book that talks about it. A hooded monk from a secret order tried to decipher it over five centuries ago, but he spent his life and eventually he came to understand only a few pages. Nobody knows what it contains and whether the pictures and signs therein come from this world or another. It's the only book of its kind that exists in which there're not only spells, but also the way to undo them. In there are locked all the secrets that life contains. No title, a leather embossed paste with the image of a big tree is all that can be seen on it. You need to know some of the things written there. To defend the truth, it is also required to discern lies. Not everyone has the clarity to discern good from evil. Sometimes evil takes the form of good to trick the unworthy ones. It is necessary you instruct yourself to be prepared for battles, but be aware, a mistake when pronouncing a spell could bring you terrible consequences, even death, so remember to pray with your heart and don't get tired to ask for good things, without taking care of how impossible they might seem.

—Where should I look for this mysterious book?

—It is inside the large Stone Vase at the entrance of a luminous cavern that descends to the roots of the Big Tree. Remember what I said at the beginning of your dream. From now on, *"one thing is your life by day and another thing by night"*. Once you discover the book, you can take it with you, but at the end of your journey, you should leave it to let it rest in the same place where you found it. No one should know where it's hidden, by that time, you'll have every word that's written on it, engraved forever in your heart.

—What else can you tell me of the Big Tree?

—Thousands of years ago a wise old man planted a seed of what would become the largest and most wonderful tree that had ever seen sunlight. It was the tree of life and happiness, with roots sunk deep into the ground, looking for the hidden water, he knew it was roaming there. Over time the delicious fruits that the tree gave were known to all the birds of the world. Thousands went across steppes, deserts, jungles, plains and seas to taste them. Soon all built their nests among the splendid foliage, living in peace and harmony for many centuries, so many that can't be counted, but eventually it came the time of drought, there was no rain for many years, then the great tree began to wither, lost its leaves, bearing acid fruits and small branches were brittle to the point of being enable to bear the weight of the nests that housed.

—How sad! Replied Jacob—. Today's world begins to fall apart with similar symptoms. In many places people are dying of hunger and thirst for lack of water. In others the opposite is true. Torrential rains drowned crops, livestock and entire populations.

—That's right! Answered Miel—, the first ones to leave their homes were the large golden eagles. Many of them returned to the steep rocks from which they came. Then followed white hawks and so on, from large to the small all birds were gone for never return. Some of the last to go were the swallows and hummingbirds. The Wise Old Man in anticipation of the drought, buried a chest in the depths of the earth with a secret to be found many centuries after his death. The ancients sought for it but they didn't find it. Some thought it was hidden in a rocky peninsula covered with salt, next to a sea where nothing lives and keeps the body of a disobedient woman. That place was once covered by lush forests, but an ancient race of giants cut down their trees and turned it into a barren and deserted land. If you find the Stone Vase and the Big Tree, you'll also find the book and find out where the chest with the secrets of life lays hidden. Would you like to look for it?

—And ... if I don't? He asked again, this time with distrust.

—You'll have a sad ending. I myself will come after you. The prize that awaits you will be ignored. You are marked with the gifts of the spirit and you must not refuse my invitation. So, what do you say?

—Yes... He replied thoughtfully—. I'll search for it, maybe I'm the only one who can find it, and I feel I've been preparing for this mission since the day I was born. You spoke of a peninsula...

—That's right; a peninsula covered with salt, which when viewed from the air resembles a horse's head. There are the roots of the Big Tree. In heaven there is a nebula that looks like the peninsula. The one here is a reflection of the one there. A thousand light years from Earth, beings from another world, carved out the shape of this peninsula for his descendants not to forget its lineage and place of origin. They came up here the only way you can cross the intergalactic space in an instant.

—And how is that done? — He asked surprised.

—In plasma bubbles. Every time you think, imagine, or do something, it creates a bubble that you don't see and it is sent into space, to a place where other more evolved beings than you collect them. They can see what you thought or what you imagined, what you did or didn't do. They are the 'decoders' but others call them angels. Not a single thought, creation, or human act is ever wasted. The good and the bad, everything is going to that place. Once the bubbles are decoded, they are catalogued and archived. When you die, the footprints of all you did it is used to define whether you are worthy for your next destination.

Thousands of years ago, people with big eyes that

proceed from that distant nebula evolved so much that they decided to get to other places and leave us their legacy. One of them, in charge of sorting the file to be sent in a sealed box inside a large bubble, while looking for a place where one day could be life, had an accident. The luminous bubble built with immense labour, exploded, the chest was opened and there came out thousands of tiny luminous beings who were inside, beginning to mix with each other in disorder and not everything was so perfect. With hard work the decoder managed to lock them back into the box and sent in another bubble to Earth the only planet he could find on this side of the universe, where one-day life might grow. But that was not the order planned by the Wise Old Man. One of those beings who would be a key in the evolutionary process mixed with other in the coffer. Unlike many things planned initially, arrived defective and would cause havoc in the distant future.

—Where is that place inhabited by the decoders? — Asked Jacob very intrigued.

—Astronomers call it the Great Nebula of Orion. If you look at the sky in the last month of the year, in the tropics you'll see it shine at the centre of the sky, forming the figure of a great hunter. One of its nebulae is known as the Horsehead and forms part of the sword hanging from the centre of its belt. As I said, millennia ago, creatures with big eyes hid the chest with the origin of life in the salty peninsula. They opened a huge hole, placed it in it and on top planted a seed brought from the nebula. Over time the seed germinated, became the Big Tree and the coffer went down with its weight. Over millennia the tree dried up, leaving only its roots embedded in the ground with the casket buried deep inside of them. To find the place where it is, you must go as high as possible and first find out where is that peninsula.

A king once dreamed of the Big Tree and ended up wandering around the countryside crazy for eight years. Since that time the huge tree trunk was cut and bound with chains to prevent them to grow out. When the king recognized the immense power of the Wise Old Man who had devised it all, recovered his sanity and his kingdom was restored. In the chest, it is hidden the secret you must discover.

Remember, you've only a few days to reach your destination. You don't have much time. Open your eyes, listen and watch, from now on things are not always what they seem, you should ask at every step the reason for each and the reason for your existence. You'll hear and see many things and must pass all tests. You are at the hour of dawn. Wake up again. With daylight, reality will come. When you'll dream again, you'll understand more. Now I must go.

Outside, beyond the wall that separates the street from the woods a lonely owl, monitors the experience from its nest in the oak tree. It lurks ready to obstruct his way, weaving in its thought a trap to destroy him, knowing that with each day that passes both have less time.

III

The cold of dawn numbed Jacob's body. He awoke with nose, hands and feet frozen feeling very uneasy about his last dream but he decided to keep it only for himself. Without still deciding what to do with the web of his memories, he felt ashamed to see the damage caused to others by his selfishness, but he also saw the damage others caused him with theirs. His life was not as neat as he thought. It would become necessary to heal all the wounds of his past, releasing the reins of his destiny. He would have to trust someone who knew better than him what to do, but who? As it often happens with humans, temptation was near and this time it would be up for him.

That morning while dictating his class, Dalila watched him as a hawk staring at its pray, without taking her eyes off him making feel him uncomfortable. Some women had this strange power over him. He could not help feeling a strong desire for her. She fixed her eyes over him as he spoke noticing a slight change in him. He leaned back in his chair and waited. Soon he realized he was following the wrong path, he decided to suppress his desires and focused on the goal of his class teaching his students about the importance of knowing how to set limits and how to differentiate between needs and wants. Then Dalila asked defiantly.

—What is your biggest need right now?

—To love. He answered without hesitation. Without love I can't be completely happy. Happiness and love are the two essentials of every human being. The two come together and they are the final aim of all of us.

Dalila said no more, she was the perfect tool to be used by the enemy to destroy him. The devil was weaving his trap with caution but he had to wait. The precise circumstances would be given later.

During the day he reviewed the lived versus the dreamed. He began to see how everything had a purpose. He'd have to change many things if he expected to reach a happy destiny. He had little time left. Miel would visit him at the end of nine days asking him for an account of what he had done or left undone. A hard road was still ahead. From the old Bible inherited from his father a statement came as a bolt coming from the past....

"The man who conquers himself is greater
than he who captures a city..."

But... where should I start? Before going to bed all was a little clearer. The root of his problems was fear, which prevented him from accepting a compromise with Crystal. Yes, fear was a pretext to hide his selfishness. It was something he'd have to decipher. Fear was undoubtedly the great blockade of his destination and housed all the negative feelings of his existence. How to defeat it? After praying, he felt a voice deep inside him that said:

"The only way to defeat fear is through faith…"

But he was very tired, he didn't pay much attention to the words and he didn't take long time to fall into a deep sleep…

He saw in his dream the huge trunk of a millennial tree and started touching its bark, moving around it, walking along its edges, followed by hundreds of swallows, but the trunk was so wide that even though he made progress, never seemed to reach to the same point. Suddenly, two fairies came in his help. They were wonderful beings with faces made of light, transparent hands and golden hair.

—You finally arrived—, they said in a chorus. —We expected you from the day Miel told us you were coming, but first you needed to find Crystal in your way. This time accept our guidance.

He observes that the bark of the tree is made with what appears to be the heads of many people coming to life when he passes by.

—Don't be afraid, the fairies sing pretending to calm him down; before going to bed you were asking an antidote to combat fear and there is only one: ¡Faith!

—Faith?

—Yes, have faith and everything will work out! With faith nothing can go wrong and nobody can hurt you. Faith is the north to get you to your destination.

But Jacob didn't know what to believe anymore. He should start by remembering the teachings of his father. Gypsies, time and taking care of multiple chores had misguided his true course. His innocence was lost the day he learned to speak and his faith disappeared with it. One of the heads, with long beard spoke with a hoarse voice out of the bowels of the trunk:

—I'm Orok, King of the Crust. I've lived here for thousands of years. I owned once a great kingdom in the same place where this tree stands now. Our greatness was unrivalled. If you risk entering its interior, following its roots, you'll discover what you never imagined, but you don't do it alone, there are many dangers beneath the surface. Some call it the 'underworld'. I don't want you to perish before you can help me. If you don't want to continue, you can stop now and so you won't risk your life, but if you decide to go ahead and free us from our imprisonment, we'll form part of your army, ready to defend you whenever you need us.

—Army? I am a man of peace. I don't need an army!

—You're wrong! When the time comes, you'll have to fight the most difficult battle a human being could face. The enemy is yourself; the path was traced the day you were born. Only you can fight this war but if you get some help, it'll be easier for you to conquer what you must. The enemy is none other than your own shortcomings. It's just a matter of time before you can see them. All human beings have them, but they don't recognize them. Make a list of them. You'll be surprised of how many you do have… start with your selfishness.

—How many of you are here trapped forming this ancient crust? Jacob asked suspiciously.

—We are thousands, millions, those who once despised love.

—What was your fault?

—I let myself be blinded by power and treasures of all kinds. My kingdom was the largest that ever existed but, on the way, I forgot to pay attention to my subjects pursuing vain glories instead. One day one of the immortals came to collect what was due to the Old Man but I had nothing to give, I kept it all for myself, so He made me part of the bark of this tree until the day that someone would release me from my prison. Maybe that someone is you. I've seen many try their luck, but none was strong enough. The purpose of those who tried was to become powerful kings as I was once. All who failed are here enclosed and form part of the bark ever since, but I feel that you are the one who can free me and in return I can give you more than any mortal ever dreamed. All you've to do is utter the words in the language of the Atlantes that are written in the cortex; you'll see them recorded on the band of my crown.

—What do they mean?

—My own name. Again, uttering it will free me and in exchange you can be anything you want. If you prefer, you can turn into a mountain of gold, or the world's largest diamond the size of a turtle shell. All you've to do is say my name first and then add the rest of the sentence that will change you into what you want to become. Start by conjuring the spell focusing in your mind the object which you want to become and add:

"Mut-A-Me-Met-A-Mu
You are me and I am you"

He went to the cortex and silently read the words inscribed in the band around the crown, careful not to utter them aloud.

—¿Come on, what are you waiting for? Shouts the king of the cortex, pronounce my name, and in return you'll get all the riches of the world. The men of old were forced by a pharaoh who built pyramids and each one turned into a stone. They have lived for thousands of years beating time and defying the elements.

—Jacob answered decisively.

"No, I won't,
Of what use are your words to me,
turning me into a pile of gold
forever condemning me to be
with no joy or love for anyone.
Your cunning is a trap,
your greed a tight knot
I'm not interested in your treasures.
Save your words and your last breath
for someone to whom you can lure.
When Miel returns,

ask him to feel like a poor,
without food, clothing, or the fire's heat,
then he may return you your life and treat
and stack you with good wine and bread."

The king begins to mourn bitterly with deep groans coming from the depths of the earth. In his dark misery knows that Jacob was brave to answer honestly to his proposals and he was not fooled by them. Slowly a huge golden salamander, merging with the shadows produced by the cortex, creeps stealthily without being detected. Jumps from where it is, aiming at Orok and rushes to devour his head. The king when aware of the danger calls in a threatening manner with all his might and tries to deter the aggressor but all is in vain. The gigantic animal plants on top of him scratching his face with razor-sharp claws. Again, the king's voice is heard.

—Stop! Who are you?

—The salamander answers surprised...

—Don't you recognize my voice? I am queen Ester, your wife; if I devour your head, I'll break my own spell. I fall hostage of the Assassins and since then they hope to come for me, but they never arrived. You were selfish and you preferred your wealth than be with me.

—Orok asks suspiciously, wrapped in sadness with his memories.

—Where is our daughter, Princess Blue?

—She's hidden in my belly and she is part of my charm. She'll not leave there until I fulfil my threat.

—Jacob is now involved and says:

—If you devour your husband' head you'll not break your spell and your punishment will be worse, losing your daughter forever. Instead, why don't you beg Miel, to forgive you for trying the elixir of revenge?

—Do you think that would work—? The salamander answers,

> *"I'm willing to try everything,*
> *I loved him once, he was smart,*
> *kind to his people as a king,*
> *but one day he began to change*
> *and greed took over his heart.*
> *I don't know if I should seek revenge*
> *or expect for Miel with his art..."*

At that moment she hears a thunder out of nowhere and a ray of light from heaven falls on the forest litter. Miel appears wrapped in flashes of light when he speaks:

—Are you willing to forgive him, ¿giving your wealth to the poor? It depends on you and if you do that, you'll heal the mistakes of your past. She responds with alacrity and a sigh putting all her eggs in the basket of hope:

> *"Yes, that's what I want the most.*
> *From now on I forgive his faults,*
> *The fact he didn't love me as he should,*
> *deceived me with his love for riches,*
> *leading me to try the elixir*
> *of vengeance and insane wrath.*
> *From today on I am willing to forgive him*
> *and share the glories and treasures*
> *of the past with the poor,*
> *being next to him now,*
> *here and tomorrow,*
> *giving always thanks for my new path."*

The trunk of the great tree begins to crackle and comes alive; they hear moans, voices and murmurs that are mixed with wind and litter noises. Other faces stand out in the bark. It's a beautiful woman of finely carved wood. Her eyes formed by two drops of bright transparent resin coming from the tree. She addresses Jacob with a sad, sweet voice, coming from the crust:

> *"I'm Balm, come, I'll embrace you,*
> *a hug will suffice,*
> *my kisses and my lips are sealed,*
> *my arms can't reach my beloved,*
> *one whom I despised*
> *and never saw again.*
> *Come; free me of my faults and abuses*
> *heal me of my tears, cutting*
> *the chains that bind me to this mantle,*
> *I never found a fault in him,*
> *his name was Malchus,*
> *I turned my back on him, I felt guilty*
> *after I cheated saying lies,*
> *but you can break me free of my spell.*
> *Come, I want to kiss you, a kiss will do,*
> *I can still be warm and nice.*
> *I'll give you all the love you want,*
> *I'll serve as your slave,*
> *anything is better than being tied,*
> *to this damn, lost and forgotten tree."*

—You deceived Malchus. Did you change his love for your greed? He asked fascinated by the voice.

—That's right. I didn't hear the call of my heart. I married a powerful man with comfort and wealth, leaving the poor one I once loved. The poor man walks alone, weeping, forsaken by all and he was never able to love another woman. Since then I found myself surrounded by palaces, treasures and dressed with lace and using wigs, surrounded by easement. Since then I never saw sunlight. That was my punishment for cheating on the poor. When I chose the rich, I became enable to love him and hated myself for having allowed this awful sin. The rich man was extremely jealous, when he died a long time after, part of my beauty was lost, my skin withered like the dried petal of a rose. I was forgotten and then my skin became hard as the bark of this old tree.

Many years passed by, but one night, Miel came and gave me one last chance. He told me to hand over all my riches to the poor in order to be prepared for the big day in which he would come and get me free. He gave me nine days to accomplish it, but I could not follow his suggestions, I loved my wealth too much. Please don't forsake me, get me out of here, let me hold on to you, I need the warmth of the man I loved once or perhaps… a kiss from you!

I can't do it, said Jacob with sincerity and frustration. He saw in her something of his own faults, his selfishness, his love of glory and knowledge. This made him ignore Crystal, the woman of his life. He saw his fear and rage to find his own face on the other side of the mirror. Embarrassed he replied:

"You lost that opportunity!
the one given to you to amend your humanity!
perhaps with some humility
you'll get back what your vanity stole from you.
That is the punishment you deserve
for becoming greedy and cruel,
by leaving the one who loved you
and never forgot you
in exchange for the riches of his world.

By ignoring love and not accepting pain.
If Miel visits you again,
tell him with humility: ¡I was wrong!
He'll know how to convert,
your wickedness, voracity and greed,
into fruits of wonder and of glee."

—But... how do I find Miel?

—You won't have to look for him, he'll find you first. Remember the lesson. Evil can't prevail over good. The good will come only when the soil is prepared and your repentance is sincere, not a second before or after.

The woman, like the king seemed to merge with the trunk, tears like hard nut shells, rolled down the bark, falling to the ground, piling on each other with a hollow sound of castanets. At the bottom of her heart weighted the words of Jacob, and then asked:

—And what are you doing here? Have you not changed the glory and praise for the woman you loved? You are as despicable as me!

—You're right, that's why I'm here. If I don't stand up to the tests that await me, I'll part of the crust in the coming days.

A few steps later, at the bottom of the trunk near his feet, the heads of two teenagers call him in a chorus:

—Have mercy on us, help us! We loved each other without knowing what love was, that's why we're here. We seek pleasure and forget the true love. We lost our way and when we wanted to find it was too late our mutual attraction vanished, leaving only the tedium born of the routine. Since then we were forced to stay together without love, but... maybe you can help us. ¿Tell us, did you ever love a woman?

—Yes, her name was Crystal.

—What a beautiful name! Did you fail her?

He replied sadly:

—I was not as honest as I should. I don't know how to make a commitment in the way she deserves it. But one night, Miel came and gave me nine days to find my destiny. So here I am in the midst of this strange path, full of dangers, questions and surprises. I can't help you. I don't have all the answers. When Miel comes back ask him to help you start in order, what you did in disorder. Then the two fairies again asked in chorus:

—Do you still wish to continue? You've not seen everything yet. You'll see many dark facets of your life and your own self. You'll have to fight to death some of the flaws that tarnish you and learn from others to avoid punishment for those defects you've not yet fallen into.

—Yes, I want to continue, I feel this is the right way...

—We can't guarantee you'll find the same path back. When we get to the bottom where the roots of the trunk end, if you find what you expect, we will not be there for you to see us and we won't be able to help you anymore. We'll leave for the 'realm beyond' because we'll have nobody else to take care in this one. By then, if you've succeeded, you can take care of yourself...

—...never mind, I'm here, I can't go back. There's something inside me that prevents it, I must begin the descent and stand up to the consequences.

—It will become increasingly dangerous, answered the fairies. —Now turn around to look, you have a surprise! You managed to free up with your answers all those with whom you spoke! Miel heard from above what you said and gave them freedom. It'll not be forever and the same hereafter depends on their actions. They will be your companions from now on. Alone you could not get to your final destination, but with their help maybe you'll do so. Now is the time to learn to work with others, trust them!

As he turned around, he found Orok, King of the

Crust. He was very tall and had a long white beard reaching his knees. He wore a blue suit covered with a cape of the same colour fluttering in the wind. His appearance was not quite human: From his eyes and body came out blue flashes of light. His sword was gleaming steel sheathed in leather studded with diamonds. His face was stern and severe, he had a breastplate and a helmet of steel inlaid with gold showing an eagle with outstretched wings and claws in attack position. His white hair escaped from his helmet reaching for his shoulders. He wore steel anklets with arabesques inlaid in gold to protect their shins, also wore leather sandals and a wooden shield with a steel rim which bore an eagle equal to that of the helmet. In his right hand held a spear, his arms were hairy and very strong. When he spoke, his voice was powerful like someone used to giving orders.

—I'm Orok the Magnificent, King of the Crust. I'm one of the last great blue kings. I've thousands of years. I govern what is now the submerged empire of Atlantis. We owned the world. Unfortunately, due to our excesses against the conquered, we attracted with our actions the 'great flood'. No one was spared, nor were traces to count our glories, the greatest empire that humanity has ever known. We were fighting men of great renown, a real race of heroes. We built channels to communicate the seas and build models of cities with circular underground tunnels that connected every continent. That was the time when we could still see the giants wandering everywhere—, he said to Jacob.

—Who were those giants?

—They were part of my people. Some of them degenerated over time, their heads became ugly and grew big ears; others developed three horns. Today the memories of their gigantic heads can be seen from the air, beneath the surface of the great lakes to the north of the great continent. A sacred book calls them *"the Nefilim"* If you rise high enough and watch like the birds you can see them under water. Legends tell that that one day they'll wake up and go out of their confinement.

—How were the holidays in your palace? —He asked curiously.

—¡Ah, were splendid! ¡In those times we held great parties! The astrologer predicted the future using the table of the oracle to know future comings and avoid miseries to come. The table was round, made of a single black stone, smooth and highly polished. Above there was a gaping hole in the ceiling. At night, the brightness of stars came down to rest on the table and the astrologer, watched their movements, like hopscotch of cosmic things to come. But one night, the stars came together to form a glowing skull with a horrible grimace and the astrologer, frightened, knew he'd soon die and the kingdom would be devastated.

—How did he die?

—No one knows, but he failed to tell the punishment that would come because of our wickedness and pride. His magic cup, always filled, rolled on the floor being empty since then and his lifeless body lay besides copying the same face he saw. I kept the cup and now I must return it to the old sanctuary which is still at the bottom of the sea, in the same place together with the bones of the astrologer. Legend has it that the day it is returned, wars will cease. I lived in the 'Palace of the Wind' at the top of a mountain, guarded by the dragons Morg and Groom. It was a wonderful place where they kept guarded all the illusions and dreams of men. Here the fairy tales hid the hopes of every mortal in search for love. Before the 'flood' came, the mercenaries, gruesome factional strongmen beings, born without feelings, able to blend with the surroundings, killed Grom. Morg escaped but no one knows where it is. They burned my palace, killed my subjects and those who survived were turned into stones. They charmed my wife Queen Ester and my daughter Princess Blue, making them, as you well know, a giant golden salamander. A few days later I found myself wandering through the fields and without any warning, coming from nowhere, Miel stood before me and proposed me with a deal: My kingdom and my family in exchange for my eternal poverty. I could not accept it. How wrong I was! Moved by my selfishness, I preferred my solitude, dreaming of recovering all my power and my wealth for myself. Many men of your time fell into this error. They became thieves, corrupt and dishonest and ignore their own families in exchange for power and wealth. When they realized they couldn't undo what they did, at that point, they had already tarnished their family name, forming part of the hard crust where you found me.

—That's right, —said Jacob. —Many kings, leaders, politicians, criminals and judges, are hidden scoundrels that move from the darkest of their burrows without considering the consequences of their actions. They believe that no one sees them, but deep in their consciousness they know that God does, so he sends Miel to take the inventory of their hypocrisy and dishonesty. Sooner or later they will be held accountable.

The king having heard these words continued:

—After nine days I woke up tied to the crust of the Big Tree where you first saw me. After listening to your words, Miel came and I, following your advice, asked him with humility mixed with fear, forgiveness for my faults and mistakes of the past, begging him to release me from spell that tied me to the bark of the old tree, therefore here I am. I'll be near you in your quest and I'll defend you and go to the end of the world if necessary, for I'll be eternally grateful to you. I also carry objects with me that have special powers and they will be useful in due course.

—Objects… powers?

—That's right, the back of my coat will drive you invisible, my helmet will give you wisdom, my armour courage, my shield will protect you from any attack, my spear will pierce the enemy's body, my sword will cut anything you want, my sandals will allow you to run like the wind and my ankle will illuminate your way in the dark. You can use whichever you think is necessary. When Orok finishes speaking, the salamander starts to transform into Queen Ester, a woman with white braids that reach her waist. Next to her is Princess Blue. The Queen is wrapped in blue tulle and holds a golden crown with three large rubies in the centre. Extending her arms, she takes one of the hands of her husband. The three come together in a tight embrace. Orok addresses him in a voice trembling with emotion.

—I've gained back my most precious treasures. As I said, I'll protect you for the duration of your trip. Mark my words from now on. Things are not what they seem...

On the side, Jacob sees a beautiful woman with a bag over her shoulder which addresses him with gratitude:

—I'm Balm, the one who changed love for comfort and wealth. My name means *"delicious perfume"* but also corresponds to a fossilized resin that flows from the bark of blessed trees. Thanks to you, Miel listened to my request. My gratitude knows no bounds. I decided to give the comfort of my palace with all my wealth to the poor. Now I am a widow looking for Malchus, the poor whom I loved once, to apologize for my abandonment and in the cold nights embrace him, heating his body with my own.

—What do you've in the bag? —he asked with the proper curiosity of naive souls.

—¡Oh, it's full of nuts! Each shell contains one of the tears that welled up in my hardened heart. Each one will keep you strong enough for a day. You can eat them when you need them.

Further ahead, Jacob sees the two lovers. This time they go hand by hand with smiling faces when they talk.

—My name is Sun and she is Moon. After you left, Miel appeared surrounded by a cloud of flashing lights. Following your advice, we expressed our desire to start in order that we did in disarray. So here we are, ready to serve you until we learn from our past mistakes. We'll help you keep order in your search and respond promptly to your quests. Don't hesitate to seek our advice when necessary.

The strange procession is complete and the march begins. Miel watches impatiently from a parallel dimension that mortals can't perceive. Before leaving, on one side of the entrance, another surprise awaits them...

When they reach the mouth of the cave, Sun warns him with the caution she learned in the school of suffering.

—Look at the huge Stone Vase near the entrance! That's the vessel that contains the memory of time. Inside, somewhere, you'll find the ancient book with an embossed leather cover. There you'll see the image of the Big Tree. You should take it with you. Don't lose it! To open it you utter the words *"Lumen Arboris"*. Remember, this is the Book of Life, no one that is not authorized can read it, under the penalty of death. You're fortunate to be able to do so.

Jacob inserts his hands into the depths of the Stone Vase but finds nothing. He asks Orok to put him upside down holding him from his feet while he searches the depths, his voice is heard as an echo from the inside when he shouts:

—Get me out of here; ¡I saw things in the background you couldn't imagine! How much time has passed since I went into the Vase?

Orok answers diligently: —Just… a moment.

—Well, it appeared several days to me.

—What did you find? —Asked the fairies intrigued.

—Several things. I understood part of whom I am and what I shouldn't be. It was a terrible experience. Locked inside are all those arrogant who lost their humility and felt better than others. Those who pay poverty wages to their subordinates, their generosity doesn't move them, only fear does. They are stingy people moved by fear, accumulating all they can. They do not trust Divine Providence. If they knew how miserable they have become or the punishment that awaits them! Those who accumulate titles, medals and merits which in reality never deserved them. They are cunning and opportunistic in everything they do. But besides the selfish and stingy, I also saw thieves, corrupt and criminals of all kinds. The Vase is a place which compresses time and space. What to outsiders seems to be a few seconds, to those inside time seems an eternity. Standing by a pool of clear water I found the book with a Big Tree embossed in the cover, when I picked it up, I felt music coming from above. I've the book with me.

—Anything else you saw? —Asks Sun shocked.

—A group of people traveling through the air on board a strange device. It was a boat resembling a huge fish, carrying criminals in its guts. Their captain looked like a seasoned pilot and from his neck hung an unfamiliar instrument. He sought direction in a landscape covered by fog. Suddenly, a seagull flew over and with his beak snatched the instrument. After traveling for many miles came to the Stone Vase and dropped to the bottom. I could see the pilot struggling desperately to keep his boat in the mist. When spinning the wheel to the right, a green sign lit that said:

"In discipline and honesty there is freedom."
When he turned it to the left, a red sign was lit that said.
"In disorder and dishonesty there is slavery."

With nothing to guide them, the pilot and the men lost their way and crashed into a mountain.

—Do you have the instrument? —the fairies ask.

—Yes, I wear it around my neck, it's very rare. I never saw one like that. It has a needle in the centre that lights up when the path is correct. I thought it was an astrolabe or compass, but its more than that, the device speaks in its own way. If I ask something it answers by turning its bars, indicating not only the direction but also a major event to come and the time it'll happen.

Suddenly the instrument marks a course. Jacob heads in that direction beginning to cross a desert. In the distance he sees a cemetery. It's very old. There are buried the bodies of the monks of an old abbey. They all have their names inscribed on stone tablets worn by time. To penetrate into the abbey, it's necessary to cross the cemetery, but a mysterious warning written on the entry stops anyone who tries it:

"You, who have just arrived
enter and read the names,
those who are buried here
once were men like you
made of flesh and bone,
who paid with pain,
their lack of love.
Search and you'll find
your name is written somewhere
you'll see it when passing by
in your dreams, late, late tonight…"

—Did you find your name? —They ask him again.

—Yes, it was engraved in a stone facing an empty tomb. I decided to spend the day in silence and meditation. I watched the stones, a flower and underneath there was a cricket. The flower said to cricket. It's very hot, the sun is in its zenith and I don't know if I'll be alive when the night comes… —the cricket answered:

—Thanks for covering me with your shadow. If it wasn't for you, I would also be dead by now, for I am easy prey for the sparrows flying on this site. You can die in peace, as did your mission. Not only saved my life but also rejoiced me with your colours. You gave peace and happiness to others who also admire you...

With them I realized their wisdom, their simplicity, their grandeur and the chain that binds all living things.

It got dark. I felt cold and fear. I crossed the graveyard and entered the abbey. At that time the moon rose, with its light I could see the bones of a pair of shaking hands, asking for help, trying to get out from one of the graves. I asked them whom they belonged to and answered in despair:

—We are the hands of a monk who didn't comply with one of his promises—. The voice of the monk left the earth at that time—. I lived for many years and died very old. When I entered the convent at a young age, the prior of the abbey made me swear vows of poverty, obedience and chastity, to which I would have to keep and be faithful. A few days after I arrived, my relatives came to inform me of my father's sudden death and that my mother needed my help to bury him. I asked permission to leave for a few hours of my volunteer incarceration and permission was granted. On my return, with tears in my eyes, I stood mute and silent until my death. Since then other monks watched how I was humble and selfless, always ready to fulfil the obligations eluded by others. Years passed until one day I died of old age. As I had no assets the monks buried me in a hole in the ground without a coffin, dressed in sackcloth and the headstone you see on my grave. The funeral ceremony was touching, since I was revered by the other monks as a saint.

—But why your hands shake so badly? ¡No doubt you are a saint!

—No, ¡I'm not! The day I went to bury my father I took off his clothes and wrapped him in a shroud, but in doing so I discovered three gold coins. I gave one to my mother, another to the poor and the third I decided to keep in memory of my deceased father. In doing that I broke my vow of poverty and consequently the one of obedience. Promises must be kept.

—Where is your soul now?

—In a dark and cold place.

—And what I can do for your soul and body?

—Unbury me! Search through the sackcloth! There you'll find the gold coin I kept. Look for the poorest you can find and give it on my behalf… Ah, my name is Alfonso.

Jacob proceeds to dig with his hands and the help of a piece of bone he'd found on the hardened ground of the tomb. Soon he begins to see the sackcloth dressing what it was once a body. Searches through the folds of the coarse cloth and finds the gold coin. Just then the skeletal hands stop trembling. Again, covers the grave with earth and goes to the abbey. He swats the door latch and waits… When the door opens, a dishevelled old woman asks in a hoarse voice and nasty temper.

—What do you want?

—I'm seeking for a place to sleep

—How would you pay me? She says distrustfully—. If you don't have any money, you'll have to sleep outside.

—It seems I'll just have to do that! I've only one gold coin, but it's not mine, I must look for the poorest I can find to give it to him—. She smiled, revealing the only tooth she had. —You've passed the test, you're an honest man, you can stay for tonight, but tomorrow you must go.

He thanked her for her kindness, had a good night sleep and at dawn he returned by another route. He crossed a forest and came to a city, the first thing he saw was a grocery store and next to it an antique dealer shop. He was very hungry and thirsty. Since he had no money besides the coin, he asked the shopkeeper if he could exchange a piece of bread and a drink for a day's wage. The man looked at him, with some suspicion answered:

—The business next door is also mine, is an antique shop and I've no one to take care of it. If you do that, you can stay for as long as you like and have food and wine to drink.

—Thanks, maybe that's what I need. Antiquaries keep the leftovers from the dead, keeping in them objects with many curses and few blessings, but… I accept your offer—. Once opened the door he heard many groans and several voices coming from a corner, then he saw a picture illuminated by a ray of light filtering through the only window in that place. The painting depicted a poor woman begging at the entrance of a church and none of those who went in there seemed to hear her pleas. The woman had three starving children, the oldest being no more than five years old. He never saw such a painting before. Next to the poor woman other ladies and gentlemen of yesteryear were inflating their breasts with pride. He listened to the woman when she spoke:

—Please sir… my children and I are hungry; could you give us something to eat?

Without hesitation he knew she was the poorest! Sought the gold coin and moved in his heart handed it to her, then said with watery eyes charged with emotion:

—Does not come from me but it comes from a saint on his way to heaven, his name is Alfonso, thank him and pray for him.

The woman looked at him with grateful eyes, her children too. At that instant he saw how the ground opened and a shining light in the shape of a monk ascended to heaven. A fresh scent of roses filled the room.

The group was shocked by his words. In each of his visions a hidden moral could be found. The stories were sad, happy or frightening, but always hid a teaching. The following visions he had when being in the Stone Vase clarified him many things.

Lit by a dim light he saw a hand, encased in a brass made mould. It was displayed in a museum and it had once belonged to a famous pianist. At night, when the exhibition closed, he came alive, gliding down from the pedestal where it was displayed, then wandered through a long corridor to reach the place where the piano he once played was also exhibited. Once there, clinging to one of the piano legs, he began climbing up to reach the keys, starting to play a sad and poignant melody. The last one the pianist wrote before his death.

—I asked amazed.

—To whom did you composed this piece for? It's so beautiful…

—To the only woman I ever loved, but she never listened to my melody. On the opening night she escaped with another man and never saw her since.

—So, what are you doing here?

—The price of fame… My body was buried elsewhere! On my death's day someone with a sharp saw separated my hand from my body to encase it the mould you've seen. Since then, my left hand is the only thing left of me.

—You're wrong… there is still your music! Of the foolish woman who abandoned you nothing remains. I can help you find the rest of your body if you fight sadness. I wish you would join us with your chords. When you see Miel just ask him to return your body and… don't think about her anymore.

At that moment I saw a maimed body. The hand in a split second is placed on it, then I heard the voice of a pale young man exclaiming with joy:

—From now on I can play my own music! I'll accompany you all the time you want. I'll let that others interpret the melody with which I tortured myself for years. Thanks for helping me out of the misery of self-pity.

Then, Jacob continues decompressing time and space, what to outsiders is a moment for him it is several days filled with strange sights.

Then he sees a red planet neighbouring the Earth where water existed once and life was abundant. He discovers an immense territory covered with pyramids, all aligned in the same direction. Somewhere in that plain, clouds of dust outline the huge head of a king. He's crowned and has an open mouth. He enters his mouth and finds that the head was a temple once so great that in its interior could hold thousands. But the most amazing thing was to meet the huge head's daughter. She was crowned and one of the most beautiful of women he ever saw. There was no difference with Earth's woman; suddenly she spoke, her voice invaded by sadness:

—Thousands of years ago, your planet touched ours. It was a shock so violent that in the midst of the cataclysm, we lost all the water. Our nights would never be the same. Since then some earthlings call us the 'red planet' but others the 'war planet'.

—Tell me more! —he asked eager to fulfil his curiosity…

Some of the water filling your planet's oceans is ours. Your moon was our sister planet.

—Twin planet?

—Yes, yes, she said wistfully. Our orbits were intertwined like lovers in an endless dance around the sun. With the crash, the planetoid that orbited us was so close, that our gravity blew it. Huge fragments fell on the surface, destroying our civilization. Somewhere there was a hole so big that all the lakes on Earth could fit into it without being able to fill it. But the worse was to come. The impacts we had to suffer were so great, that all our volcanoes erupted at the same time, its ash blanketed all. Since then huge storm dusts sweep our surface.

—But... did anyone survive the catastrophe?

—Our scientists predicted that all this would happen and took the necessary precautions. They built huge caves where early life was stored. A handful of our people survived, hiding under the surface ever since. That's why today we have big eyes unlike the earthlings. We had to use them to see better in dim light. Earth could not escape the cataclysm either. Huge waves covered your planet and large earthquakes buried entire civilizations in unfathomable depths below the surface of the sea. All volcanoes also erupted. That was the time of the Great Flood. Such was the darkness that you could touch the dust suspended in the mist of vapours. Have you heard about it elsewhere?

—Several sacred books speak the same. That was the time that coincided with the collapse of a great civilization that some call the Garden of Eden, others Hesperidia's Garden and still others the great empire of Atlantis. Now answer me: Who dwelt first in our solar system?

—We did, —answered the head. We are millions of years older. At some point we visited Earth starting a beneficial exchange between us, until the Great Catastrophe obliterated everything. We were a race of wise beings and invented the 'sacred geometry' which we took to your planet. There is only one planetary species. We are all brothers and come from the Horse Nebula in the Constellation of Orion. It's just obvious that we are alike but some of the changes that make us seem different began millions of years ago. Regardless of the differences that led us to adapt to different environments, we'll be part forever of the same species. Don't forget!

—You mean the inhabitants of earth and those of your planet can have children if they so wish?

—That's right. In fact, they had and will continue to do so.

—Why do you tell me all of this?

—To clarify many questions to scientists of your world. Also, theologians, for in your Bible is written that there will never be another Great Flood. The reason is simple. There's nowhere from where the earth can get more water. What this book tells is that the waters raised several 'elbows' above the highest peaks. That means that the volume of water that existed at that time was three times higher than the one now exists.

—And... Where did all that water go after the Flood pass?

—It was lost in space, slowly evaporating. Someday, sooner than you think, humans will arrive to our planet and discover that we are equal. As a matter of fact, humans have already arrived but that is a secret that hasn't been revealed yet. Earthlings should follow our example and hide under the surface to survive. It is urgent to do so, as they have done in the past and in the near future it will do so again. You are our most trusted emissary to tell them to follow our advice. Again, I repeat, don't forget, the future of the earth is to learn from us. What happened here will happen there again and this time the fire will be the great destroyer. Then the cold and dark will come and as the sacred books says, everything will be renewed.

On turning to look away he was dumbfounded: found himself in a metal, solid, compact world, where the atmosphere had the feeling of being precise, dense and cold as metal. His voice didn't produce any sound at that site. Giant bubbles flowed up from the bottom of a lake upon breaking in contact with the surface, producing very fast alternating flashes, with colours mixed on the horizon as reflections of an endless kaleidoscope. The banks were covered by white sand forming desolate beaches. In the midst of this bleak scene he saw an ice giant column slowly emerge from the lake and a woman tied to it by what seemed to be two snakes with strange reflections and red scaly skin dotted with black spots.

—Say my name, save me! —The woman cried in despair, —only you know how to do it! Shouted again... Moon whispered something in his ear, and then Jacob answered:

—You're the one with no name. The one that was neither cold nor hot, you were neither good nor bad, only lukewarm, that's why you have been denied entry into the higher circles. Even if I wanted to, I do not know if I can help you. You did nothing for yourself or for others. Then the woman screamed in terror and the column began to sink slowly.

—Save me! She shouted again. Then he heard a splash, turning to look he found one he hadn't seen before.

—Who are you? He asked distrustfully

—I'm also called the Acheron, the ferryman of death. I told you at the beginning of your dream I might seem like many things. Look at my boat, it has two oars, you can use them if you want, I've not come for you yet, now try to rescue the woman, but first you'll have to answer to the serpent.

—But I see two of them, both tying the woman to the column.

—You're wrong. It's just one with two heads, one at the beginning of its body and one at the end. Things are not what they seem to be.

Wasting no time, he pushes the boat and jumps into it and starts rowing towards where the woman is. The column continues to sink slowly. When he approaches to the column one of the heads gives a breath and says.

—Say my name and I'll let her go!

—You're the indecisive, so you've two heads! He answered it shouting from the boat. —With one head you deny what you affirm and with the other you affirm what you deny. You never knew what to choose, or didn't let others help you.

The snake released the woman before the column sank completely until it to disappear beneath the waves and then she cried.

—My name is Sofia, —she explained gratefully, —in the world there are many people like me, indecision is the daughter of insecurity, I hope my experience will be a lesson to all those.

But the things he saw didn't end there that day. On turning to look back, he found something that froze his blood. The body of a man wrapped in a cocoon was poking his head out. He was imprisoned and enable to move when Jacob heard his muffled voice plead in a desperate tone:

—Please, please, get me out of here!

—Who are you?

At that moment Moon said something in Jacob's ear.

—I'm the naive! He replied ashamed—. I married several times looking for a comprehensive woman and the only thing I did was to meet those who were only interested in my prestige, power, pleasure, or even money. Of the women I've known she's the worst and she is known as the 'Black Widow'. Shhhh! Hide yourself! ¡there she is, lest it devours you too! The first thing she does is to inoculate her venom and when you are paralyzed, weaves a cocoon around you. Inside lays her eggs, so that little by little, when their young are born, they can be feed upon your body.

A giant spider with a female's head and fangs descends from the web pouncing on him. As he is prevented by Gen, not to touch any of the sticky threads of her murderous web, jumps to one side and asks her terrified:

—Who are you?

—I'm the 'Black Widow', others call me the 'manipulator', I am dedicated to fool gullible people like you to draw them into my web, once there, when my eggs hatch, they will devour you in a long and painful process. At the end all your blood will be sucked, your flesh consumed and your skeleton will remain stuck to my web forever. You have no escape—. Then he shouted with all his might.

—Miel, hurry! Come to our aid, save us from this horrible widow!

At that moment, the spider in the middle of horrific screams it's burned by lightning coming out of nowhere and the man in the bud is released. He's in his middle ages, he has a thin profile, aquiline nose, and his eyes covered by thick black eyebrows still have a lot of expression.

—Thanks, my name is Jacob, I'm a writer. I'll follow you wherever you go in gratitude for having freed me.

—You owe me nothing. Jacob responded pensively. The next time you fall in love with a woman, you mind that she's virtuous, lest you from getting caught between her threads and this time no one can help you. How many times have you failed?

—Many, so many that I lost account. On the way I discovered that my faults attract those which are no good to me. My intentions are sincere, but not those of the ones I meet.

—Maybe it's the other way around... have you thought about it?

After a long silence he answers

—At the moment I'm better alone and I have no strength to try again. Tell me, do you've an honest woman in your life?

—No, I once had one. Her name is Crystal. Then Jacob asks puzzled:

—What do you write about?

—About life—, the naïve answers meditating every word…

—However, she's death not important to you?

—In my case, I prefer life, this wonderful gift of which I was not aware before the horrible experience I just had.

—You're right, sometimes you've to die in order to appreciate life and start living. Now follow us and write about everything you see and hear. Many can learn from your words. I think Miel is expecting it from you...—Wait, I hear a voice coming from the grave—... Next, he asks: —who's there? —In the midst of total darkness, he hears an answer with an echo behind him:

—I am the mummy of Ramses II, a pharaoh who was the greatest among the greatest, the owner of the world at that time, of the Nile to the right and to the left, of life and death. Then a deep guttural voice was heard to echo within the Stone Vase:

—I was buried in the Valley of the Kings and inscribed all the monuments of Egypt with my name. I was a tomb's destroyer if it didn't bear my name, I was the inventor of chariots and light cavalry. I hunted lions in one of them, I cut heads with my sword, my grave is the most visited of them all, Abu Simbel is so important that mankind after millennia, it had to pay a tribute to move it from where I built it. I thought I was a god, but one day I discovered that I wasn't.

Then Jacob asked him with curiosity: —how did you find out you weren't a god?

—I had a horrible toothache, and then I realized I was made of flesh and bone being a mere mortal like the rest of my subjects. I felt a great disappointment when I find out. I would like to leave my confinement and reconquer the world. Get me out of here, lend me your body, I promise to change your life for death, and then you'll be eternal, like me…

—Sorry, I can't do it. I am looking for my own destiny, but you instead, found yours. I wouldn't like to see myself in a museum, locked inside a glass casket preserving me from flies and curious hands... Tell me; were you happy when you had it all?

—No. The toothache always stayed with me, my queen died young, the eldest of my sons was slaughtered in a disastrous night at the hands of a mysterious angel sent to punish me, my kingdom was eventually conquered by a neighbouring country and I was forced to sign a shameful peace, my army perished beneath the waves of a stormy sea, my grave was ransacked, its treasures stolen like my body, my heart and my brain. All that remained of my greatness is this embalmed body, filled with jewellery, where the tooth is still causing me much pain. I am the last human vestige of an era that had contact with a great prophet who spoke with God and the sea. Please get me out of here, who knows, maybe you can go further!

—No, I can't get you out. A heartless man loses everything. On the other hand, you were never the greatest. There was another who came after you and he was. The mummy gives a shout and begins to disintegrate in the midst of horrible grimaces and his ashes are swept by the wind. All that remains of its greatness is a tooth laying on the ground as a mute testimony to his pride.

That's what he told of his visions that day. He had many other experiences but chose to keep quiet. At that moment he felt a thud and he was found face down with his head bobbing in the air, his body sustained by his feet by one of the powerful hands of the giant Orok. Next, he goes looking for the book embossed with the image of a big tree which he'd found at the bottom of the Stone Vase and yells with all his force:

"Lumen Arboris!"

The book and the trunk of the great tree seem to come alive. The cover is illuminated with the image of a tree and a river of fire runs through it. The bark of the tree begins to twist and crackle as if to be liberated. A very narrow gap appears leading to the unknown, through which all of the birds penetrate. In the background is what looks like a cave with light flashes. He senses that his destiny lies down among the roots of the Big Tree and cries again:

"Lumen Arboris!"

The book' cover ignites again, and then he opens it and asks:

—Where is Malchus?

In blood-red letters an order is written:

Only Balm must read it!
"Ubi tu Malchus, ibi ego Malca."
- "Wherever you are Malchus, I'll be your Malca"-.

Balm reads the words, then she hears a flash and a being made of star dust begins to form out of nothing. It's Malchus. Balm hugs him and kneels to his feet. The man lifted her tenderly saying with gratitude:

—Thank you, everything is now in the past, I forgive you. We both grew up with the experience. The future holds better things for us if we accept our daily mistakes. The past is our greatest treasure; we'll have to return to the dark spot where we started and move forward on from there. Being honest with our feelings gave us back our life. Feelings make up the true reality of every human being.

The descent is about to begin. No one knows what they'll find below. They are at the entrance of the luminous cavern. A forest of stalactites and stalagmites are so closed to each other that forced them to go around without breaking any. They are the souls of those being filtered like water, purified, touching the floor of the cavern, forming bright and fantastic shapes. Some already reach their ends forming columns. The wind crosses howling with moans and scary sounds. The procession is about to enter the underworld, a place revered from ancient times, where Orfeo, the king of poetry and sad music roams. Orfeo is looking for his dead wife whom he dearly loved; he's playing his lyre in the hope of finding her and if he does, he hopes to revive her with his chords. But all is in vain. She is no longer there, she became dust and disappeared centuries ago. Orpheus wanders alone, he's lost and nobody knows where he is. Only his music and poems sometimes are heard coming from the depths…

○○○

Slowly, the light grows dim, the descent begins, they see a woman who has two halves and the group listened to a dialogue between them. The one facing the front is the light and the one facing the back is the shadow. The dialogue goes like this:

Shadow: "—I'm so quiet that I sometimes think I don't exist."

Light: "—But you do! You simply can't see itself!"
Shadow: "—I envy you. You are so beautiful!"
Light: "—that's one of your problems: Envy is a big part of your dark side. The other six Capital Sins also reside in you: <u>pride</u>, <u>greed</u>, <u>lust</u>, <u>gluttony</u>, <u>wrath</u>, and <u>sloth</u>! You are never satisfied! You occupy more than half of the universe, you are the reverse of things, the calm and rest of men but you are ungrateful! You are almost infinite; your rage resides in that you were created!"

Shadow: "—Thanks to me, things aren't seen. When they aren't seen no one knows they are there. It is as if they didn't exist..."

Light: "—But they do! If it weren't for me, women couldn't see themselves in mirrors, jewellery wouldn't shine, works of art would never be created, trees wouldn't bear fruit, flowers and colours couldn't be seen and men and things would never wake up. Look how easy it is to turn off and disappear instantly, but when I'm turned on you go elsewhere and watch me in silence."

Shadow: "—what are you trying to say? Without me, lovers couldn't hide, secrets would not exist. Many fears me and confuse me with evil! In me there are hidden thieves, murderers, alcoholics, addicts, liars, all forms of violence, dishonesty, selfishness and corruption that exists, as well as all those who don't want to show their faces or to be recognized!"

Light: "—that is the worst of you! On the other hand, I don't like secrets; we have as many secrets as we are sick and we are sick as how many secrets we do have. At the end everything will be known, secrets will cease to exist and only love will shine, the light, me! Now shut up...listen, someone is coming down! I must be turned off and disappear. You can cover it all with your shade..."

Jacob exclaims amid the darkness:

—I hear women's voices. Who's in there? At that time, the room lights and half of a beautiful woman speaks decisively:

—It's me, the light. The dark and I can't share the same instant but we can share the same space… in spite of being always together. Henceforth I'll light up when you call me only during night hours and in your dreams if you shall ever need me. I'll be at those times when you live what you never understood of the spirit world and your own emotions. You won't need me during daylight, sunlight and the heavy reality of every day will be enough. None of us here can live during the day, only your memories of the living world, the hard bustle of every day which humans use to make their living with. Now I must go, the lanterns fairies bear with their hands will suffice for the descent and help you see many of the horrors that lurk in the shadows of this place.

Suddenly the light turns off completely and the shadows wrap it all with its mantle. Jacob can hear the footsteps of the group rumble against the stone walls. Each fairy carries a lantern in one hand putting flashing glitters on the roots hanging from the ceiling, like mouldy tentacles, raising flocks of bats begin to fly erratically. Every time he steps on a rung a piteous groan is heard. Jacob stops asking the fairies:

—Who moans in that pitiful fashion? —They answered in unison, like two tuning coordinated diapasons.

—Those that are tread on the descent.

—Who are they?

—Those which are hurt when we step on them.

—But you haven't told me their names yet!

—The proud ones! Which are tied up to the rungs. Every time someone treads on them, allows them to break their pride. —Suddenly a cry is heard.

—Get me out of this spell! I'm tied to this piece of stone because of pride. My heart was hardened and I could never look down to the neediest, who I should have helped. Instead I looked up towards the top. I envied those who had more than me. When I reached the top, I didn't have anything to envy from no one, I felt better than anyone, and I forgot to be grateful with life and walked away from all those around me. All you've to do is to hit me so hard that I'll break into pieces… at that moment my spirit will be set free.

—What are you willing to give in return?

—I'll give you power over men to dominate them at your leisure. You'll own their cravings and nothing will be done without your permission, —Jacob growing wiser every time, responds with decision:

You failed in the answer!
I'm not interested
in your power
nor your cravings!
You are Epulon, the rich man
described in the Bible,
your offering annoys me
your words too

> *I don't need your crumbs*
> *I prefer sincerity,*
> *the flame of the heart,*
> *the love of a family,*
> *the song of birds,*
> *or a loving hand.*

The descend continues in what it looks like an endless spiral, while the cries of those still locked into the rungs remained behind. As they move, they realize that for some is the end of their journey, while for others is simply the beginning. The fairies stop at the threshold of a closed thick wooden door. Rusty metal hinges of old wrought iron suggest that something important is behind that door. This is the first of the doors to be crossed. The two fairies still carry lanterns in their hands and let them rest on the tiled floor. Hidden behind the roots, as if from nowhere, a long and lean gentleman whose forehead was crossed by a dark vein that stained it as if it were a soot, he speaks with a booming voice that echoes in every corner of that room.

—Why have you come here? All who crossed through that door died or were lost and never found.

—Jacob boldly flaunting replied:

—I came here driven by my curiosity and moved by a warning of life and death. I've no time. I am looking for my destination...

—Did you find it?

—No, not yet.

—Can you help me?

—The man gives him a huge ring from which it hangs a heavy iron key. Then he adds moved by Jacob audacity:

—Enter alone; I'll wait for you outside! You should answer without hesitation the three questions that each of the three beings who are chained to the bottom of the enclosure will ask you.

Before he enters, he puts Orok's helmet on his head, which immediately adjusts to fit the exact size of his skull, his ideas are clarified and courage gain momentum. In the thick gloom, shadows seem to cross fast from side to side, sliding down the walls. The two fairies and the rest of the company stand behind him. A deadly silence invades every corner. In the background he can see what appears to be three large blocks of marble and tied to them with a strong chain, three burly men seem to come alive and awaken from their slumber. The one to the left, is the hypocrite, who first asks hoarsely with resonances filling the cavern.

—Who am I—? Without hesitation Jacob answers:

—The one who is not what it seems to be and pretends to hide his feelings. You are the deceiver!

—What animal am I like?

—The chameleon, you hide and camouflage behind the truth hurting everybody around you with your lies. You are selfish and only care for your own benefit. You discredit others nurturing from the damage you do to with your razor-blade tongue.

—Which is my favourite flower?

—The poisonous orchid. You are an androgynous being. Confuse and fool everyone with your appearance. You aren't sincere but false, a liar and envy eat your guts.

At that moment the being gives a horrendous scream and the chains that bind him squeeze him to the hard marble suffocating him even more. Then is the turn of the ungrateful.

—Who am I? He asks with a wince of pain.

—The one for which the benefits received don't match the expected gratitude. You suffer one of the worst spiritual defects that exist. You're not even grateful with your own mother. The greatest scorn is the lack of appreciation for yourself or others.

—What animal am I like?

—The fox. You're sly, selfish and treacherous.

—What is my favourite flower?

—The nettle. Woe to those who cherish your beauty, your bite will soon feel like the sting of a serpent.

Again, a deep groan, coming from the ungrateful entrails invades the enclosure and tightens the chains on his chest. It's the fool's turn.

—Who am I? —He asks in a choked voice.

—The one who lacks the judgment to distinguish truth from falsehood and justice from injustice. You are insensitive and can't see or feel the evil in yourself or in others.

—What animal am I like?

—The vulture. You feed only on carrion and the misfortunes of others.

—And… which one is my favourite flower?

—The autumn flower! You can't survive nor in wealth nor in poverty. You're good for nothing. Parts of you are poisonous and produce allergies to those who approach you.

Again a cry of pain fills the air and the sound of suffocating chains are heard when the fool is squeezed hard against the marble.

Jacob gives a cry calling the light. The room lights and he hear the voice of a sweet woman.

—Here I am, look closely around you. —The three burly men begin to merge with the marble blocks until they disappear completely. In the background, behind the blocks three doors can be seen, each smaller than the other. The fairies repeat in a chorus:

—Use your wisdom and what you've learned. Choose only one of the paths you'll see when you open each one of the doors. If you're wrong, you could die or it'll be more difficult to reach your destination.

Once he opens them he sees three different landscapes. The smallest door has one hidden path covered with the leaves of old trees, moss and giant ferns. It is the longest of the three. It crosses rivers and waterfalls, but wild beasts lurk in the shadows. The median door when it opens leads to a road not so long, planted on the sides with shrubs and small trees, however what it seems not to hide any threat, is a hoax, there are hidden venomous snakes and it nests treacherous tarantulas. The largest door shows, once it's opened, a narrow path. It's the shortest way but without no food or water. It crosses a burning desert where black poisonous scorpions wait for anyone who walks in there. Finally, he decides to take the path beyond the smallest door. He opens it and the fairies yell in terror.

—You choose the long way!

—Yes, —he answers, but the most resourceful. There is water, water is life and life. All are love.

They all begin running through the woods and haven't gone far when a two heads black wolf faces them with a howl. —Our body is made of anger and my heads are called intolerance and impatience. We can't be one without the other. Prepare to die. The animal displays threatening huge tusks in each of their heads, bends its ears back and has goose bumps of the spine. Without hesitation, Orok throws his javelin with such force that crosses the wolf's heart in a split second. It's still dark, but dawn is coming soon. Jacob hears wrapped in echoes Miel's voice:

—It's enough for today, when the sun rises you should wake up. Soon it'll be a new day and you'll continue to work in the world of reality and the living. Your students are expecting you and they need you.

That was the end of their journey that night. Outside, the menacing owl stands on the wall across the street with his back on him, as if despising his efforts. The remaining time is getting short and his destiny seems to escape from him.

When Jacob told the monk of all his experiences with Miel, he described in detail the bitter—sweet pain when the spear pierced his chest and when it was withdrawn with his entrails hanging, tangled on the tip. Then he showed him what he wrote and when trying to read his own scribbles, a torrent of tears overcame him choking his throat and moans filled the room, touching the monk to the deepest fibres of his being. The monk realized that an angel had performed an exorcism to his friend. In plunging the spear through the heart and removing his guts, the demon left by Tania as an inheritance had been expelled escaping with a dog's howling. He remained silent and didn't add anything else to avoid scaring him further. He knew that upon the devil's return he'd have to be strong in order to resist temptation or oppression. He was accustomed to these battles born from the depths of the soul. Steadily turned to one side of his bedroom and pulled from his library's shelves, a book of blue pastas and worn edges, there was stressed all which Jacob needed to know and read slowly:

"...The saint wrote her memoirs, at the direction of the Fourth Angel, but the other three had also visited her as a child; the first was the Angel of the Lance, capable of producing pain from the heart and a deep bond with the Creator so that never again she could live without Him despite her sins. The second, the Angel of the Rope, was commissioned to make a loop around her neck leading her whenever in straight path; the third the Angel of the Rock, was in charge of crushing her like a worm with a heavy stone of trouble in order to bend and remove from her any trace of pride, and fourth the Angel of the Burning Arrow that pierced her heart inflaming it with the flame of love..."

Of the remaining five angels, the book went into details

he'd not mention. Jacob's mind was fixed on Miel's glowing eyes. The monk put his hand on his head, saying he hadn't a thing to fear. If that had happened to the saints, it could happen to anyone. Someone strong was looking for him, and then offered to give him absolution for his past sins. The monk knew his friend well and that beautiful women were his misfortune and Achilles heel. The poison left by the gypsies was still in him. If he'd ever loved Samira, that love was in the past. His one true love now was Crystal; however, over time he realized that his destiny was to live alone. He could not accept the idea of a compromise. The love he tried so many times only left behind contrails of pain.

On his knees, with tears in his eyes, in an act of gratitude he received absolution and with immense pain he accepted the words of his friend and confessor: He'd have to choose between God and Crystal; he could not live with her without marrying her if he wanted his sins to be forgiven. But not with her or any other woman he'd ever marry. He'd never change his status. He thought he loved his freedom and solitude above everything else and he had a deep fear of establishing a relationship of commitment 'to the grave' after his bitter experience with Tania. That day, he thought later, he made his worst mistake. He knew men played love to find sex and women sex to find love, but among them, sex and love were always the same thing, an expression of love; however, the priest's instructions had been precise and simple:

—If you won't marry, you don't do her more damage! Let her go and don't look back...

With these final words began his great battle. On one side was what the church preached, the church where his mother had him baptized snatching him from the devil, and on the other was what his instincts dictated, but at the end, fear of being excluded from the circles of heaven was decisive, so he decided to go for the teachings of the monk. He consulted the swallows his decision and they replied that in their kingdom there was no church, they were all united by instinct, but in the case of humans, a battle should be fought. Each man was the sole author of his eternal destiny.

IV

That evening, instead of going to his house decided to walk alone in the park and he could not help thinking what he'd say to his last and true love, the one she had after Samira. The tone of Crystal's voice made him sigh. The memory of her skin and pearl hands caressing his body made his blood boil. The thought tore his heart. He wandered who'd be the saint to invoke at the time and remove the temptation to call and get her again in his arms. A saint had withstood temptation jumping naked on a rose bush full of thorns and so had overcome his desire for the woman he loved, other had felt the sting of the flesh with great force and another prayed. "Give me chastity whenever you want it but, hopefully don't give it to me yet..." Maybe that was the answer, chastity yes, someday, but not yet. Without thinking more, briskly walked to the attic where Crystal lived.

She'd learned to walk with firm step her world around and it was difficult to discover she was blind. Her blindness was acquired suddenly at the age of fifteen. She still held in her memory the basic colours of the rainbow although some had diluted slowly. The tone of her parent's voice was also treasured and she feared that soon it'd be completely forgotten, because that would sink her into an even deeper darkness. She loved being told stories that mentioned them or be described the colours of pictures if brought to a museum. She could walk unaided without a cane several blocks around, and the whole neighbourhood knew her and loved her soul and eternal smile. Sometimes she was accompanied by Sarcasm a huge grey dog Jacob gave to her, and he explained to her that the name in Greek language meant literally 'to tear flesh'. The dog looked like a mastiff with a nasty temper, but it was meek as a lamb. The city was indeed a dangerous place and more than once it protects her by its mere presence.

He had keys to her apartment and he could wait if she hadn't still arrived. On the way he bought her a rose and rye bread that was her favourite and decided to tell her he loved her, at least for the last time before he had the strength to leave her. In the solitude of the kitchen he thought again about the words of the angel, he still had a few days to pay bills and settle his affairs and then took a momentous decision, perhaps the most important of his life. He'll leave her forever. She hadn't arrived yet. He once wrote her a poem as part of a story and read it to hospice's children. In it he told the loneliness and sadness of a bewitched princess. The poem had a secret hidden that only a prince that with the touch of his hands, could turn ugly things into beautiful ones, would understand. It read like this:

"Search, search that you will not find me
If you come to my house, you will not see me.
Under the tree
I will no longer be.
I am close, very close, but you cannot touch me.
Search, search, that you will not see me
Alone in your soul, I will always be.
Weep, weep, but you will not reach me
Soon, very soon, I will have to leave...
Under the tree again I will be.
If you come to my house, you will not feel me.
Leave me a loaf, a kiss and a rose
Only in your mind you will find me,
and only there you can love me.

Search, search that you will not find me..."

She placed the poem as a premonition, in a sandalwood little box, the only inheritance she had received from her mother that contained a rose, a tuft of hair and her milk teeth. Also stored in there were other pieces of paper with Jacob's poems, a few coins she didn't spend in her days of fasting and saved to give it to the poor. Every time she opened the box, the scent of sandalwood escaped in the air and brought as a gift her mother's image and a rose with her lover's kisses. He visualized her weaving in the kitchen, in the empty seat in front of him and asked her what she was weaving his time. She answered that she knitted time, each node was a second, in every second was a knot. She wove a sweater for him. Wove it in the same way spiders do when spinning their cocoons. A sack made of invisible knots of time. She continued weaving, wove thoughts, wove the music she was hearing from the old kitchen radio. She wove with her eyes, moving her fingers like the spider, also using her mouth to count the knots of time. He wondered how he'd feel when dressed with thousands of seconds, every thought into a knot, and every note of music chained to the other. He left the rye bread along with the rose and the keys on the kitchen table and with a sharp pencil, leaving grooves in the paper so she could read them with her fingers, wrote in the book of recipes:

I love you... I won't see you anymore...

On his way home he was shocked of he'd done. Perhaps the monk would be now satisfied and would surely appreciate his sacrifice but he wasn't sure he did in getting any peace. His decision was verging on the edge of madness. He looked and examined his feelings, his torn selfish heart, which had prevented him from marrying the woman of his life. Began looking at the back of each mask and saw what he really was. The outer face was the false part of his image, one that everyone saw. The truth of what he was the inside, the back of the mask, the part that stuck to him, the hidden part that only he could see and he didn't like what he found. Then he thought the outside of the mask was the best, but in reality, in the depths of his being knew that it was not: the more polished and decorated, it was farther from the truth. The inside of the mask was the mould of what he really was… or perhaps of what he wasn't.

Rid of all the details that hid his image became a painful process about which he once wrote. The first of the masks was his own skin, the file of all his feelings, of all the caresses of those who'd loved him. The parade of his mistresses' defile to the sound of his own footsteps on the cold pavement of the street and realized that the caresses of Crystal's hands were the only ones that mattered. Then he meditated for a few moments and tears came to his eyes. Her memory was always with him as a thorn in his entrails. He wanted to call her covering her with kisses and to apologize for being so blind, but that was something he could no longer do. If he'd called her, he'd have to ask her to marry him and that he had ruled out since the first day. Marriage was not his vocation, the monk was right, he would have to let her go and not look back. His life belonged to the world and not to a woman and that was the way it'd been marked by birds from the time of birth. It was necessary to feel his own pain and grow in it, accepting his new reality. Urgently he felt the need to write; sought his notebook and let the ink flow as his own blood on the white paper, feeling relieved in doing so.

When she got home it was dark, moonless and freezing cold. She was accompanied by Sarcasm and had a premonition that something terrible was about to happen. She made her way to the kitchen. Felt the faint aroma of Jacob's colony and her heart pounded, full of hope. Any sign of his presence made her heart beat with unusual force. Felt perhaps he was there. She called for him, but no one answered. Passed her hand gently on the kitchen table and found the reason for her fear. Read the note written in the book of recipes letting the tips of her fingers slide smoothly over the grooves left by the pencil, the message was below the last recipe she had prepared him: chicken livers and rice with dried tomatoes. She didn't touch the rose for fear of plucking the petals. Rye bread and the keys were left in place where they were, as a memorial to the love that wasn't and a tribute to his memory. When she opened her sandalwood little box heard a mysterious music coming from nowhere and voices that seemed to call her. She could see her mother looking for her as a child and remembered her kisses and caresses. She took the parchment paper folded into four parts containing a withered petal, a poem written by him for her birthday she knew by heart and sang it silently, then wept bitterly and her blue eyes turned like the sea. In the darkness of the room Sarcasm bent its ears, crawling on the floor, felt the deep loneliness, the sadness of her soul and began to lick her feet.

She felt a chill and in the kitchen's darkness with Sarcasm's heat warming her feet, recalled her experience with the exorcist, the mysterious monk and Jacob's friend. In the days when she gained more confidence, she proposed him to be subjected to an exorcism. His past was thought-provoking. The matter with Tania, his strange gifts and failed relationships were sufficient indications that something was wrong. They requested a meeting with the monk and they went to see him. She entered first into his office and told him everything about her past. An hour later the exorcist blessed her, gave her absolution and she went down the hall to where Jacob was expecting him. With a silver bucket in one hand and a sprinkler on the other began to recite prayers in Latin and wet him with holy water. He fell on the floor with a thud and a pitiful cry came out of his entrails. The demon of sadness brought by the gypsy's curse still haunted him, but the angel of repentance and sympathy was also there. The Exorcist continued to pray and when he finished asked him with compassion:

—Want to confess? I know you can't talk, just shake your head as a sign of repentance.

The Exorcist had the gift of clairvoyance and closing his eyes began to tell his life's story, giving dates, names and details he didn't even remember, or that only he knew. When the monk spoke of those sins against love, he opened his eyes as if seeing something on his mind, then advised him with concern:

—When you go home tonight, look in your books and hidden there, you'll find four which you must destroy. —Four hours had passed since the exorcism began; finally, Jacob's throat was clear when he asked breathlessly.

—And... What should I look for?

—Look slowly, then you'll find four books of black magic. One is of ancient rites and gypsy curses, two are of horoscopes and the third is related to the Tarot cards. —He realized that these books had been Tania's, leaving them there. The Exorcist went on. Also destroy your mask collection, wooden statues and pagan gods. There are twelve in total…

—Why should I do so?

—These objects are acting in your life as antennas to attract the evil one. Remember, tonight destroy them all! I'll be praying for you to avoid any harm. Now go and do what I said.

The exorcist knew that while Jacob had sincere repentance, his purpose would not last long, but he gave him absolution anyway. Would be with her again and while he didn't have the strength to leave her, he could not ask for more from a human being. He saw a pure love between them, a one that was better to let it flow like water and knew that no one on earth could judge them.

When confession was over, Jacob accompanied Crystal to the attic where she lived and walked with a firm step to his house. Obeying the order of the exorcist, the first thing he did when he arrived was to search for the four books on magic. In reviewing his library remembered his life. There was all of it, frozen in the words of others, words who were already his. A book of home recipes that his father always kept in the cart, taught him to clean the marble with olive oil and to keep ice crystals between two glasses. There he learned the recipes for poultices of vinegar with a sprig of mint to reduce fever and how to dye Easter eggs for getting canaries with seven colours' feathers and was quick to apply his knowledge to the swallows. One day he found how to write with a pen and Chinese ink on the shells of freshwater crayfish and decided to make a necklace to Samira. He bought a wicker basket, filled it with them and could not sleep that night with the sound of castanets produced by crustaceans' legs wanting to escape. Samira discovered them and they ended in a memorable flavoured soup.

At the top of his library, he found his dictionaries and encyclopaedia's collection. Some were thick and some thin, some he bought and others were inherited from Vincent's. He liked to read in them names' meanings but never found his. The Divine Comedy was there, the love sins of Paolo and Francesca made him sigh and instilled fear. If they had gone to the second circle of hell then very few would be saved, only those who'd known true love. He travelled with fingertips the titles of his books and a flood of images escaping from its pages came to life. Heroes, martyrs, saints, beggars, rivers, mountains, hidden valleys, battles, tears, joys, sins, symbols, animals, roses, sighs, poems, stories and secrets that led to some unknown adventure. Tucked away in a corner, he found one book that wasn't his, camouflaged, as if waiting not to ever be discovered. It was the book with black magic and ancient pagan rites and he shivered. He continued looking. Beyond were the two horoscopes' books, one with the twelve zodiac signs which included the mysterious rites to celebrate the first day of spring; the second a manual to invoke lost spirits. Hidden, behind an encyclopaedia he found the book of the

Tarot. He remembered Tania and her yellow eyes. He lit the fire and began to incinerate them as ordered by the exorcist. The flame grew; it became huge and began to devour the pages of each book as a hungry beggar. Then he could not but think of hell. After, searched all his twelve statues of wood and did the same. Each one fuelled the fire, in a mystical ritual of purification. He was afraid and tired, his eyes were swollen from smoke and the stress of the afternoon's tears and decided to go to sleep. It was midnight. A flutter awakened him, jumped and stood beside the bed. It was three o'clock. Steeling himself took three steps toward the door of his room. Turned on the light but saw nothing. He felt a rumble outside. With the help of a flashlight, he looked into the shadows in the direction of the noise. His studio's window was open and when he lit up the lamp on his desk, he saw standing there two yellow phosphorescent eyes, fixed on him. A huge owl looked at him with defiant angry eyes. He went to find a blanket to trap it but escaped through the window into the cold air of the night and landed on top of the white wall across the street.

The day after the exorcism rose late, feeling refreshed in spirit. Put on his turntable blaring a fandango's guitar concert and he decided to take a bath. He let the bathroom door open so he could listen to the concert and after a few minutes noted with surprise that the room was filled of a very thick black smoke. In running the shower curtain, smoke enveloped him completely and he could not breathe. He thought he'd suffocate. His house was burning! Naked, ran like a madman, looking for the fire everywhere and when he reached the fire place, to his surprise found it was off. He opened the kitchen's door and saw an orange blaze coming out of the floor, igniting the wooden roof. With a towel soaked in water dulled the fire, he went out and lay on the floor. He was exhausted. When opening his eyes, he felt cold and saw Crystal's face, her hands stroking his forehead. After the dreadful experience he ran to his house, called the exorcist and told him what'd happened. He seemed calm on the other side of the line when he spoke:

—That was an attack... you know from whom… I stood praying for you all night. The enemy is furious to be banished from your home. Don't fear, the worst is over.

The time of sunrise was approaching fast and she still was in the kitchen with Sarcasm asleep at her feet, thinking she had lost everything that nothing mattered, that life without him would never be the same. Burst into tears that began to fall as thick drops on the table and felt a deep loneliness. Suddenly she heard the flutter of an owl in front of the attic's window. Sarcasm pricked up its ears and growled. The owl went away, it came to the Jacob's window, hit the glass hard with its beak waking him also.

The first rays of sunshine came when he opened his eyes. Once he did, the owl went away again and took refuge in the oak tree. She never ate anything again from that day offering her fast for him. The rye bread remained on the table untouched and the rose stood fresh with no desire to die. Perhaps love was keeping it alive.

Before giving his class that morning, Jacob decided to seek the monk and tell him more about his dreams, but this time omitted the details and what he had written. He feared that his friend would consider him crazy and that he no longer be in his life to explain the meaning of his things.

—Be patient, said the monk, —I think you're in the process of purification. You have something to offer and much to receive.

—I don't understand anything, why me? I'm a small thing and I have little to offer. I'm so selfish and I lost Crystal by refusing to marry her. So far, I have not been able to understand why you demanded so much from me. Tell me, what should I do to not lose her heart? I would like to return to her and say it was all my mistake, a trick of fate.

—What little faith you've! God is an unequivocal being and so are his signals!

At that time Jacob recalled the angel's words. He was instead an equivocal being and things were not what they seemed. He'd have to ask at every step the reason for his existence. Then the monk saw in him something that made him think. Whatever it was that was happening, the enemy would also be ready to conquer and would use every means at his disposal.

—Are you protecting yourself with prayers? —The monk cautiously asked.

—What do you mean?

—You need to pray more than usual. The enemy is on the prowl. Sometimes he's disguised. Have you noticed something strange in the last few days?

—Yes! —he said surprised, —sometimes a shadow follows me, sometimes a huge owl with yellow eyes haunts me and scares the swallows that are always around me. —The monk explained urgently:

—Well those are some signs! Maybe he's hiding as a shadow or in the owl scaring the swallows. Good and evil can't coexist simultaneously in one place, as well as light and darkness can't either. When one arrives, the other one leaves—. With that phrase he remembered his dream from the night before and knew with certainty that the monk was part of the chess game to his destination. Without hesitation asked him again hoping to discover more…

—Tell me of another signal, —the monk replied:

—Sadness. Don't you see? The evil is always infinitely sad. When he's around the soul is also sad...

MIEL

Santiago Martinez Concha

V

That morning Jacob would teach his students, among other things, that in discipline and honesty there is freedom. That would be a good start to teach them become into what they should be. He'd avoid love talking. He still wasn't sure if he'd understand the word and if he'd love again. When in the same class, Dalila, the smartest student asked if he believed in God, he answered with certainty and in doing so, without realizing it spoke of love:

—It's easier to believe than not to believe. Whoever denies Him and thought of Him he seeks for Him. Those who seek will find. No one can talk about Him without somehow believing in Him. —But… Dalila was not an easy person to overcome.

—God doesn't exist; she said in a tone of pride and mingled irony. He went out of fashion. Today, hardly anyone believes in Him, only the sanctimonious wearing rosaries with odour of old incenses. The modern world is sufficient unto it and is evolving at a pace that keeps you from seeing. How do you imagine God?

He seized the opportunity given by his student and replied fixing his eyes on her:

—Open your hands, raise your arms to heaven as I read something that I've in my pocket, it won't take long, is shorter than eternity … It's my…

GOD'S IMAGE:

To do,
to undo,
to re-do,
alone
in time,
floating in time,
seeing the universe,
from time
flowing,
running,
going between
the paths of infinite,
back to the time,
time,
time looking at God,
God looking at time,
supreme dialogue
infinite dialogue
incomprehensible,
eternal monologue,
tireless
necessary
simple,
acts of making,
of unmaking,
acts of being,
acts of knowing-how-to be,
acts of power,
of love,
infinite love,

to break himself,
being alone,
alone,
over time.

When he finished, his students were silent, Dalila's arms tired and she asked forgiveness for her pride, but deep in her heart continued to nurture her plans. That morning it also taught his students something different. He spoke of a secret. He was focused in the story of a mythical king named Orok and his wife, Queen Ester. For many millennia, when a great continent was still showing over the waves of the Atlantic sea, a huge ridge divided it into two. The most surprising thing was that from the top and due to the sun's position, one of its sides remained in shadow until noon and the other did the same in the afternoon. Then the giants that lived there decided to embark in one of their greatest works, using the occasion carved a dragon along the vast land mass and along its shores. The result was terrifying when viewed from a great height, as the great dragon seemed to fly with the movement of the sun, leaving America and landing in Africa and Europe. But something fatal to mankind came. Men and giants turned from God, beginning to revere the great dragon. In the middle of the monster's head was a beautiful oblong plain and also at it's the centre, the most fantastic city ever built by man, surrounded by a stone wall lined in gold could be found.

Unfortunately, their king and his subjects were interested only in accumulating wealth and riches at the expense of bringing all the conquered people to slavery, becoming despotic, cruel and selfish. This drew the wrath of God sending a flood with furious contractions of the earth's crust, which plunged the great continent forever under the sea's waves. His students listened spellbound, when finished speaking Roger asked:

—¿Are you talking about Poseidon, the one carrying a pitchfork when the Flood came? The one who went down with the empire of Atlantis and of whom mythological stories tell he had a chariot pulled by dolphins?

—Yes, the same. He sank together with his people because of pride. That was his punishment and it is something to remember. Pride is the worst of all the human masks. We are only masks of what we pretend to be, imagining being, or are sorry for not being. From all, the worst are the proud.

When the class ended, he said goodbye to his students for that morning. Roger came speaking softly in a mix of fear and timidity:

—I've to talk to you, perhaps if you've more time… Something is torturing me. I don't know when it would be the best time to talk to you.

—What is it? He asked with curiosity.

—It has to do with pride, but I've fear of talking about it and that someone can hear me. Maybe now is not the time. — And saying this he left with tears in his eyes...

Before noon, Jacob went to a downtown hotel in search of a sauna, seeking to leave his back pain, soaking his body in eucalyptus' saturated vapours. On the road made a list of all his grievances. Maybe if he could get rid of them, he would get rid of the termites eating away his spirit and his back pain would disappear. He thought about who would be the first on his and soon found them. Some had fallen into the inevitable corruption brought by the century's decline fall and with the anguish of the winds predicting the end. No one seemed satiated with anything. One of those who had met at a symposium invited him to dinner at his home and there, boasting in front of him, opened his huge safe where he stored dozens of gold ingots. He felt compassion and a deep disgust with the fact. He realized the man's gold was stored as a 'fear's product' and not as a 'love's fruit'. The sole purpose of his secret wasn't to help others but to satisfy his greed and his own fear, anticipating some misfortune in the future. Jacob knew he didn't have a happy ending. What were once delicious roasts ended up swelling his belly and accumulating lard in his arteries A few days later he died when his heart broke, and couldn't take even one of his gold bullions to the grave! No one cried. He thought that those people who committed the seven deadly sins walked freely through the world and of all those like filth floating in the sea of debris, some were committed by those who had been elected by the naïve to command them.

Other culprits of the destruction of morals, customs and the sins against faith, were committed by many priests whose actions claimed justice to heaven, but there were a few like his friend the monk, whose hands were clean, being able to offer sacrifice at the altar. The monk did always the best without expecting anything in return. The latest in the list were those who used injustice disguised in the mask of justice. All these children of greed were smarter than the naive children of light and were responsible for bringing humanity to ruin, scamming people and nations with promises and practices of usury never seen before. Basically, all were guilty... but the worst was he, when he thought how he had defrauded Crystal's love and confidence.

Love had disappeared in the majority and was it hidden in the empire of fear, anger and heartbreak. Greed, greed, lying, crime, greed, lust, jealousy, envy and licentiousness were touching the limits of the ninth circles of heaven. Soon, according to ancient traditions, no stone would remain unturned, no safe place would remain and no place to hide. He'd decided not to read the paper in order not to absorb the bad news. In his meditations on pain he asked himself why the ups and downs of his life. Most lived flat existences; nothing extraordinary ever happened to them. He wondered if everyone should pay their share of pain and what was its measure. Eventually he found the answer: pain was made as a fingerprint, different for every human being. He could not measure the pain of a human being, or compare it to the pain of another... it was as important recognizing hunger in one poor man, as to recognize the same hunger affecting millions. He also discovered along the way, that pain is the perfect tool carving each man to his own size. Then he thought he could not get to heaven without passing through the filter of pain. He wondered if there would be any pain in heaven and concluded that it was, other than the physical pain, just in the spirit and therefore deeper. If that were so, how much pain there should be in hell?

Santiago Martínez Concha

VI

Lost in his own web of thoughts he continued his painful descent to the hotel's ground floor where he arrived looking for help in the form of a massage and the heat of the sauna. He thought of Dante, one of his favourite poets, when he fell to the deeper basements of hell. In there he saw, confined to the Hypogeum, the desperate, the hypocrites and those who by their example and scandals dragged others along. Suddenly came to his mind memories of his last night's dream. The copper railing helped him on his descent, holding to it as an invalid to his cane, with a sore back growing ever stronger. When he reached the ground where the massage room was, a dim light illuminated a pair of agile and strong hands waiting for him. The hands of the masseuse began to slide down his neck and back, infusing the skin with orange oil. Her nimble and expert fingers began to find his muscles gimped as hard knots, undoing his tensions and easing his thoughts. In this entire welter Crystal was a safe haven and one of peace for his soul. He thought of his favourite poets and heroes which were all made with proper acts born of the deep roots of generosity. Once therapy finished, he sought his notebook and he wrote his last meditation, it frightened him when he read it again:

PAIN

Perfect tool with sharp teeth,
of unfulfilled dreams,
lost illusions,
broken hands, crushed bones,
affronts without hesitation,
toothless mouths,
tearful faces,
children washed by tears
of injustice and neglect
empty bellies,
lost innocence,
silent screams,
cold nights,
forgotten dead,
wilted flowers,
desecrated graves,
soldiers ignored
mourning those killed,
those without parents,
the nothing,
the miserable,
the poor, always poor,
those that cause pain,
criminals,
heartless evil men,
ruthless jailers,
dirty minds,
stained souls,
coward spirits
abominations of the past,
mistakes of the present,
forced orphans,
futures discarded

desecrated dead,
severed limbs,
Abortions without cause,
causes aborted
throats slit,
eyes gouged,
those without hands,
without feet,
the museum of the death,
they can't kneel
because they have no legs,
they forgot the forgiveness,
mutilated women,
men laughing in dark corners
ruthless monsters,
mangy dogs, war stories
philosophers of lies,
preachers with insatiable greed,
of lust, envy and wrath!
¡So much pain!
When will the desired day come?
The day tears will dry
and dust will cover all your clothes.
When will the sun of justice,
come and obliterate injustice?
When will it shine in a different light?

But evil had its own plans and its time had come. That afternoon Jacob sought for Crystal and didn't find her. She wasn't in the attic or in the cloister. He looked for her at the market where both enjoyed going but she wasn't there. He asked flower sellers and papayas' but none gave him any reason of her whereabouts. He went by the convent, the plaza and the hospice and he didn't see her. By late afternoon he found her behind the wall, facing the woods, looking empty, sitting under the oak's shade with the sandalwood box in her hands. Slowly he approached without touching her. The fragrance of his cologne came to her like a sigh come from afar. It was the same as ever used by his father and remained her the smell of lemons and limes from the hot lands. She asked with a sad breaking voice:

—What are you doing here? Please leave me alone, I need time to understand. The confidence's cord broke and now it's hard for me to trust you. You asked me not to look for you and now you're the one who does it. Let me go, my path is marked and always will be. You discovered that I am one-man woman—. He felt shame and selfishness. For a moment he felt a deep hatred against the monk blaming him for their misfortune but realized that the culprit was himself. His friend had acted in good conscience, following the dictates of faith, practicing what he thought was best; embarrassed he answered:

—I don't know what to say. I ruined both our lives. I came looking for you and now that I did, I know it would be wrong if I go back to you. I was just moved by my selfishness and the love I still feel for you. Get it? In my dreams I've seen the same thing happened to others and the punishment they had to endure.

—Yes, I understand, she told him sweetly, thank you for having the courage to come and tell me in the face. I know it hurts to see my sadness, fortunately I can't see yours, and I can only listen to your voice. At that moment he felt mortally wounded and a sword of ice pierced his soul. He reminded Miel eyes with his spear in hand, their guts hanging out and the little time he'd left.

—I love you, love you forever, I still have a few days. She didn't understand why he said that and asked him in amazement.

—A few days for what? What do you mean?

—I'm not sure... To find my destiny, I don't know what

it all means.

He told her of his dream with Miel and his talk with the monk the day after, then he wept bitterly as a child, with an unfathomable sadness. She felt his pain and although she could not see his face, she understood everything. Like the monk said, they were both part of God's chess.

Don't be afraid, —she replied, —I'll help you. Next time I'll look for you, for now wait patiently to see what He wants from us. Everything is written ... Say goodbye from me to your sons whom I've learned to love them like they were mine. I love the small adult with his jokes, he'll always be in my prayers and you too. Now go my love, leave me alone, I need space and time…

He held his head in his hands and was sobbing; when he turned around looking for her, he didn't see her anymore. She briskly left quietly, stepping on the moss of the forest, disappearing without a trace. He felt again the void in his heart. An owl hovering in the top of the oak looked at him with hatred and dropped some feathers in its frenzy's flapping.

With an opaque sun about to set on the horizon, on his way home he met Dalila, standing in the middle of the empty square. She was alone when he saw her. She noticed his sadness and invited him a cup of coffee and he accepted nodding his head. Dalila always felt drawn to him, but she knew it was an impossible love. She was twenty years younger and he could be her father, but his stories fascinated her and decided to explore his grief:

—Tell me your sorrows and I'll tell you mine, —she said, but he didn't feel much like talking. No one would understand, only the monk and of course Crystal. But Dalila was a woman who never gave up easily and being his teacher, he knew that. He realized they both wanted to be with each other. He was about to fall into the trap and be overcome by temptation, he felt a knot in his gut and asked bluntly:

—Will you come?

—Where? —She answered as if pretending not to know.

—To my home, I don't want to be alone for reasons that perhaps you intuit. If you come, I want you to stay there overnight, I still have some time to find my destiny, and maybe you are a part of it... I don't know.

At that moment he could not measure how certain his words would prove. She felt a deep desire to be with him, she lived alone and she had no reason to give anyone an explanation to whom she'd spend the night with. She was young, impulsive, and beautiful, with bright eyes like burning coals, black hair like thoroughbred horses he once saw in a town's fair. She was full of life and had a sense of humour that everyone enjoyed. Her body hadn't a thing to envy Crystal's and her hands either.

Yes, I'd go, even if you don't love me. Perhaps on the way you could, —she added hopefully. Then, gathering what little honestly, he had left in him, gasped with doubt:

—Don't expect that I'll, I've a broken heart, but right now I need to share my loneliness and sadness, I can see my own selfishness now. I hope you come. —But by then both took a bite of apple's desire. She touched his face with one hand, and then she replied:

—I envy the woman you love; I'd like to be her.

On their way to his home, they passed Crystal's attic and saw the kitchen's window ajar, he felt the remorse of the hypocrite in him Dalila realized his shiver and said instantly:

—Don't look up, at least not today! I'm with you. If you prefer love me just one night. One night is enough!

Crystal had said the same the day he met her. They came home and Dalila bluntly said:

—Make me yours now!

He, without any tenderness, like a wild animal, endorsed it. When she felt his skin against hers, she gave a cry of pleasure:

—¡I finally conquered you, you're mine, tell me what you want me to do and I'll do it!

They looked like two squid in the water, in a dance without end, until they fell asleep exhausted on the room's old Persian carpet. The cold awoke them at dawn and an owl hoot, standing on the window's sill looked at them with scorn. He recalled the angel's words... *"Things aren't what they seem to be..."* He felt a deep shame, remorse, saw his hypocrisy and that he wasn't better than anyone. He had betrayed Crystal's love. He knew that in the depths of purgatory's circles bordering the walls of hell, the hypocrites were locked for all eternity; they were the worst of those condemned. Humiliated and fearful, next to this woman whom he didn't love, silently he wept bitterly his own defeat...

Next morning, he got up early, looked for the largest bottle in his kitchen he could find, he decided to go to a church and fill it with holy water. The monk was right, he needed protection from the enemy. Dalila was awakened with the noise, he hurt all over, they didn't speak and they not kissed. They had little to say to each other. After a cup of coffee and a two days' bread, it was time to say goodbye and Dalila asked sensing his response:

—Will I see you again?

—No, not in the same way, but I'll see you in class. Sorry, I know that this time selfishness and desire got the better of my principles. I can't love you like you deserve it, because as you intuit, I gave my heart to another. After being with you, I think I should resign my university's position.

No, please, don't. It'll be our secret. I'm satisfied with it ... As long as the secret remains, I'll always have something from you.

V

St. Ignatius' church to where he decided to go was in the city's centre. With a bottle that could contain two litres of holy water, he got on a bus and began meditating on the road the events of the night before. He felt empty and guilt invading him. Where was his love for the woman he loved? How could he be able to behave that way on her backs, taking advantage of one of his students? The sun awoke the city with its noise and ever-changing landscapes. The smoke and coal's gases soon invaded his lungs. As the bus approached the centre he began to cough.

He remembered with nostalgia the countryside and sunrises in Vincent's wagon. Suddenly he realized the valley of sorrows around him. A crippled lottery's vendor sat next to him. A secretary later revealed a broken pair of heels and nylons pulled half way up, she probably didn't have time to dress, she had spent the night with her boss and was feeling like Dalila. Two beggars were fighting for a coin. The driver gave the people orders to move towards the back of the bus. He saw when a thief's hand took a lady's wallet and he escaped using the back door. The driver slammed on the brakes and two gentlemen, perhaps his accomplices were left to pursue the thief. Soon the bus was full of people and it became almost impossible to move or breathe. A pungent smell of sweat took the environment. Certainly, the enemy was everywhere pinning all its talons and he had been part of his game the night before.

On the way to downtown, his mind took refuge in the day when Vincent told the story of his family. Mercedes, his paternal grandmother had long hands, streaked with blue lines like river maps, wearing always a black horn with a silver trim around her neck just to hear what interested her. Vincent lived with her before he met Ruth. Mercedes also instilled in Jacob devotion to St. Ignatius. If he prayed to the saint at night, as a reward she'd prepare him delicious desserts: figs in syrup of her garden, curd with syrup, baked apples covered with caramel custard topped with blackberry sauce, lemon peel sugar plums in juice or dessert of cream with raisins, and its favourite: passion fruit foams and the floating islands, for which she used an enormous tray, where the egg whites served with powdered sugar, floating on a yellow sauce adorned with chips of cinnamon and everything wore a sprig of mint and a lemon grass and said that these herbs attracted good spirits and cured any ailment. One day, during a revolution, she died of old age. His family had two graves in the crypt of St. Ignatius' church, a sort of catacomb located under the main altar. There Mercedes ended up, buried without even the dignity of the box; in the midst of the revolt, funeral homes were closed and the few existing caskets all were with a body inside.

One day his father took him to see her grave, they went down by a grey small marble staircase to one side of the altar and at the bottom of it, and a fence separated the living from the dead. Opened the iron's fence door and entered a tunnel. That tunnel was another of Jacob contacts with eternity, it led to a maze of vaulted whitewashed walls decorated with wild flowers painted on them. He was impressed by air's freshness in a place that seemed to have none, but somehow the monks who built it centuries ago, managed to create an air current. Felt a strange pride to have a grandmother and his uncle Henry buried at that site, one of his father's ten brothers who never married.

Henry was a neurotic, napped after lunch with open doors overlooking the house's patio decorated with pots planted with hydrangeas and geraniums, lay down using a black dress, wearing a tie the same colour and a collar shirt, black hat placed on his knees, straight legs in stockings and black shoes also after joining the heels pointing the toes toward the ceiling of the room, closed his eyes and placed his hands' palms on his chest. He looked dead or praying as Jacob was watched him in silence. At six in the evening he got up, it permeated his hat down over his eyebrows and brandishing her umbrella like a sword, he left the house to chase the prostitutes who used to seek their prey in a neighbouring street where he lived and who never managed to seduce him with their charms. He gave a medallion to the nation's museum, recalling with this gesture, his great—grandmother, a woman who suffered pain testing. Over a hundred years before, someone wrote about her the most famous love story ever. Jacob had inherited from his father a few of the writer's letters and his picture showing an enormous moustache, and in the back a dedication with his signature.

Another of his uncles was Peter, who wrote stories as a stone rosary strung on a string. To him and Vincent he owed his love for old things, a taste for the countryside, words, attic with kisses and passionate hidden secrets. Of the other children Mercedes had, Mercy died as nun, Elizabeth married a musician and she was happy, she had ten children, but none could bear the surname. Florence died unmarried drinking in a dark tavern called Mesopotamia; Hippolytus operated himself of a gallbladder's stone, opened his stomach with a razor blade and bled to dead. Joseph died of old reading in his library, he married a cousin and both were sterile. Eunice placed inside her house's balcony a huge cage with hundreds of budgies and blue feather canaries she'd domesticated to sing when they felt her presence; over the years

she moved politically towards the left and gave shelter to a
guerrilla leader priest. One morning, the cage door appeared open
and Eunice disappeared never to be seen again. Yet neighbours say
that after freeing the canaries she fled with the priest. Dogbert, one
evening in a nearby river went for a swim, he was sucked by a
swirl and his body never found, Antonio died in Australia and no
one ever knew what he was doing there.

Joseph, who was a dentist, one morning, came to his
office's door, a dreams' seller, loaded with calendars; he came with
a toothache on a new motorcycle. At the sound Joseph went to the
door and the seller could see the patients' queue in the waiting
room. Then he offered to give him a ride around the block on his
new device as long as he didn't make him wait. Joseph who never
rode in one of those devices before was excited to the
extreme. Wrapped in his white robe, sat on the back seat and for
the first time in years felt free as the wind and on return, grateful
stuck out the seller's tooth. The seller, who always wanted to be a
dentist, proposed him with a deal: the dentist's office in exchange
for his bike to which Joseph agreed. As an added bonus he also left
him with his wife; she was frigid, and saw him from the door, he
dressed in his white robe, leaving behind a stars' dust cloud. Years
later he died on a trip on the Arabian's desert, and since then
psychiatrists know this escapade as Joseph's Syndrome.

At noon, carrying the holy water's bottle in his hands
he attended a teacher's funeral from the same university where he
taught. Amid the ceremony and funeral songs, he'd goose bumps
and once again felt the guilt of his sin the night before. The
ceremony ended, he went to his house and sprinkled holy water in
every corner, leaving half the bottle's content on his desk in case
the evil or Dalila without notice decided to return. In the evening
he visited the cloister and pleaded with the monk. He was tired and
exhausted. Continued his inventory and in reviewing most of his
life he realized that he still had things to do. He opened the
bedroom's window and the owl with its wings grazed him, but this

time he ignored it, he leaned back in his bed and fell asleep without being able to move. This time he didn't write anything in his notebook. The owl was happy and looked satisfied inside its nest in the oak tree... it'd won another battle and time was getting shorter...

Santiago Martinez Concha

VI

That night Jacob went to bed thinking how sad his life was without Crystal and wondered if the devil would have something to do with it. In the mist of his memories and the battle of his soul, he thought about of the man with the wide—brimmed hat he saw that afternoon on his way home. There was still some time before sunrise, he fell into a deep sleep and had a vision. He saw himself staring ahead on an endless straight path illuminated by a full moon, suddenly he saw something coming, first a dot, then a silhouette against a colourless background. The figure moved slowly but he was unable to stop it; the figure went through him and kept walking. He realized the figure was Crystal's. They were back to back, looking in opposite directions, both weeping bitterly. At that moment Miel appeared again and said with a clear and forceful voice:

—Jacob, rise with the breath you still have and watch! You have much to do yet! Don't rest! Keep looking! You have little time left! Learn from everything you hear and see! Don't be fooled! Yesterday you didn't finish your dream's tour; we need to do it today. You'll have to purge the offense committed with the woman whom you don't love and concentrate in the one you do. You must leave the forest and start walking through the desert. —Then he answered embarrassed:

—Why do you harass me? In this journey I find a

solitude that seduces me and that I hate at the same time. It's like going to war without worrying losing my life. I would like to kiss Crystal, see my children, mourn alone, sit by the river and feel the tree's shadow I once saw as a child, hearing the swallows singing, playing in the wind, hearing the targets' call and see my grave in a sunny day, knowing my body isn't there, that all was a war I dreamed with. — Again, the angel looked at him in a mixture of compassion and authority.

—One thing is what you want and another what is expected from you. You must be brave. Would you like to be part of the Big Tree's bark, becoming one of the stone steps, or being tied to a marble's block? Death, like life, has to be deserved. Now continue with your journey, I guarantee nothing will be wasted! Pain is the only tool that will cut you to the exact size of what you're. Pleasure instead distorts the view of yourself to make you think you deserve everything without merit. Don't waste your breath; you still have a long way to go before reaching your destiny.

At one point, the road forks and everyone stops. They have reached the deepest place in the forest and no sign of what is the true path that will take them to their destination. Then Balm looking worried says:

—You have reached the trail's "Y". Every living thing ever comes to it. Last night you chose the wrong trail and everyone will have to suffer the consequences. You can't give your back to what you did before or hide the sun with your hands pretending it is night, but don't fear, everything has a solution, don't lose hope. Sometimes it's necessary to return to the point where we made the wrong turn and start all over again. Let me explain. Some years ago, a rich and lucky man, decided to try a forbidden elixir; such was his fascination and the state of euphoria reached ingesting the brew, that he preferred it to his wife, his children and his wealth. Over time, his wife and children felt relegated to a dark corner of his home, sad and abandoned. Soon everyone left including his servants and not even the dog, once his friend, wanted to stay with him. But the man cling to the elixir and nothing in the world could stop him. Things got worse. Feeling alone, the elixir became his only solace and consumption increased. By neglecting his business, their riches were gone and considered ending with his life. But one day a true friend decided to listen to his troubles and gave him a message of hope.

—What you told me, is nothing new, —said the friend. —Happened to many others too. All you have to do is think about when your life changed and start over at that point. —That's exactly what he did, he broke the bottle keeping the forbidden elixir and he began to help others; this time giving of his time was all he could do. When his wife learned of his efforts and she saw he was trying for good to make a real change, she came back to him and his children too. The man recovered the good judgment, his family and his wealth, thanks to a special grace he received from someone greater than himself and a true friend.

—That's simply a wonderful story—, replied Jacob…—it has a happy end, I wonder what'd happened if the man hadn't abandoned the elixir…

—He'd probably died alone in a hospital, the street or a jail's bed…

The march continues and he asks Miel's guidance in taking the right path. They begin to notice the place becomes muddy, trees begin to lose their greenness and freshness, huge toads and snakes come their way, but he dodges them, leading the group without using Orok's sword. Soon, the swamp water dries, only sand, stones and dust remain in the middle of a sweltering heat. After a long stretch, they begin to climb an endless hill. It's a painful climb with no water or anything to eat. When food is gone, Balm comes over and offers her nutshells' tears.

—Come! —She orders impatient. —It's time to use

them. —He gives his companions first, then eats the leftovers. The two fairies whisper their secret in his ear:

—We are identical twins, water's daughters; we can help quench your thirst. The thirst you feel is the thirst of the spirit. You were trapped for a long time in a spiritual desert. Gather your hands making a bowl with them. —Water flows formed by liquid tears spilled by the fairies filling them. He again invited the others to drink first, then, he drunk slowly to not waste a single drop, when all finished they said satisfied:

—You've purged your fault and overcame your selfishness, but left consequences that can't be revealed yet. This time your repentance is sincere. The signals are clear and well defined. Sharpen your senses. When time comes, you'll understand. A big surprise waits you at the end…

MIEL   Santiago Martinez Concha

VII

From the top, Jacob calls the light and immediately illuminates the landscape. Below they can see the desert, the forest and a lake reflecting trees with a strange glow.

The lovers Moon and Sun turn to him with a warning: That's the forest and desert we left; we should go down this side of the mountain facing new dangers. In a cave you'll see along the path, dwells a three headed giant. You should go alone inside the cave and prove your courage; the giant will try to step forward and kill you. You should tear him down and cut off one by one each of the heads with the sword Orok left you.

—Who is that giant with three heads? —He asks terrified.

—He's the selfish one. The higher head is himself, that's the one you should cut first. The second coming out of his chest is the cruel which has already eaten his heart, the third is the insatiable eating his entrails without ever satiate. Each of them will make you three questions before attacking. Don't believe their promises. Use the helmet from now on to get wisdom and have the sword ready. —Seeking for another way to escape the Giant's encounter he replies with fear:

—I've never killed anyone! I don't know if I can do it...

—It will be your life or his, you should not hesitate or you'll die!

The march continues. The descent down the slope

begins in silence, hurting their hands and feet with sharp rocks. Below they could see huge round stones that seem planted on purpose where they are. Their tops resemble large animal backs with buried legs in the earth. The fairies speak quietly.

—Be careful not to touch any stone, those are the Monsters, relatives to the Assassins. Each represents a character flaw. The largest is the one who's asleep in the cave. Contact with any of them will awake them from their dream coming to life; we have no way to defend ourselves, there are too many, waiting for someone to pass by and accidentally touch them, its function is to watch the entrance to the cave where the giant, is king and lord lives.

Carefully the party avoided touching any rock but something unexpected happens. Balm's bag becomes entangled in a rocky sharp edge and then she falls precipitously against the stones. Jacob realize it and without losing a moment calls everyone to hide under the immense Orok's cape, there are silent. A vast army of hideous ogres slowly awakens to life. A stone shaped with huge walrus tusks incorporates itself and screams loudly:

—Who dared touching me? —Jacob leaves the cape discretely while the others remain under it motionless and unresponsive.

—Hey You! Go call your king and master, lest he be offended because you killed me without giving him the pleasure of doing it himself!

A huge circle formed; huge animal's forms surround him preventing any escape. A monstrous shaggy hair rat with a long tail and sharp teeth speaks with shrilly voice:

—You must wait, for even when he sleeps, none of us would dare to go in the cave and awake him. Mercilessly would devour the first to do so, but instead, if you want to take the risk of going by yourself and wake him up, we wouldn't stop you from doing it. It would be a good show to see how you deal with him.

—Make way! Jacob says with flaunting authority. We'll see how smart and brave your king and lord is!

The animals caught with his attitude open a street for him to access the cave. It's a huge, dark place covered with bones and full of twists and turns. When he enters, thousands of bats wake up making crying with a deafening noise. He reaches a central space whose scope is immersed in darkness and he calls for the light.

—¡Come on, come on you must give some light now! It's urgent to do so!

In an instant the cave is lit and he is horrified by what he sees. Laying on the soil, the skeleton of a headless man is holding a sword with his bony hand. Thousands of other bones and skulls are scattered across the floor. The ceiling is magnificent and it is carved into the rock, revealing gold arabesques like vermin of all kinds moving quietly as if alive, holding to the edges of the rocks, as if they had suction cups on the ends and were about to drop on any intruder, such as spiders stalking their prey do. The space is circular and surrounded by doors leading to various sites of which only one leads down to the centre of the Big Tree's roots. Hidden in there, a pond guarding the chest of life wait for him. Thousands of gold coins and bullion, jewels of all colours, chests pearls filled, with gold and silver trays with carved handles, jugs and vases and fine monogrammed tableware and old silverware, shields, helmets and armours inlaid with fine metals studded with rubies, emeralds and diamonds. Bronze and marble statues, are piled up in disarray. Lying on his wealth, a giant awakens with the light, his booming voice echoing throughout the cave:

—Who is so foolish as to disturb my sleep not knowing my name?

—You're wrong! I know your name, you're the selfish and the one with excessive affection for yourself. You've never loved anyone and never will. In your cave, you can only live together with your ugly heads and useless treasures, surrounded by your selfishness which prevents you from sharing.

—What is my favourite metal between gold and silver? —The Giant asks satisfied, thinking this time he won't get the right answer.

—You like both but prefer platinum, the most difficult to get. The one you have is in the form of a ring you once gave to a woman, her you loved her; eventually despised her throwing her out in the street, snatching the ring from her finger.

—What is my favourite cup made of? —This time the Giant asks with rage.

—Diamonds. All you have never shared them with anyone and served no purpose. The ring you gave to the woman, set in the platinum ring, you kept it as a souvenir of your contempt.

—You're a dead man! —growled the Giant; ¡before you answer to my other two heads, you'll have an end that don't quite imagine!

A second head comes out of his chest. Its bloody fangs showing that serve to tear flesh; a horrible grimace with a rotting stench can be felt when it shouts:

—Who am I?

—You're the cruel, unbearable, violent, hard and bloody. In you live one of the evilest germs that exist: Violence! You'll have no pardon for your crimes if you won't repent on time.

—What is my favourite metal?

—You love two: iron and gold. With the first you put your mark on the burning bodies you tortured; with the second you made a cup in which you drank your enemies' blood.

—And my favourite cup made of?

—…the most common of all things which is found in

the sand you stained with the blood of those saints and gladiators who spilled it in the circuses' arena of ancient times: Quartz!

Then a piercing roar is heard coming out of the Giant chest's centre. It's the turn to the insatiable, the worst of them all. A fat ugly head comes out of its bowels with his intestines hanging from the mouth, dropping them when asked:

—Who am I?

—You're the insatiable. One who never manages to satisfy his hunger or thirst! Every time you want more and more, never share with anyone your food or drink and never satisfy your ambitions. Some confuse you with greed, but your real name is gluttony! You're addicted to everything! In you live the desire to acquire and accumulate food, drink and wealth. From everything you've saved, you won't be able to take anything, only the groans of the poor asking for justice.

—What is my favourite metal?

—Lead, which is the heaviest and makes you feel you have plenty.

—And is my favourite cup made of?

—Salt; with it you increase your thirst and can't ever calm it. There is a lost tribe whose traditions speak of a man who ate a pan of salty rice. Such was his thirst when he finished eating, he drank all water from a huge jar in the house where he lived, then went to the village's well and drank all the water that was in it. But his thirst was still unfulfilled, drank water from a stream that crossed nearby and then the entire region's supply of river's water, until he reached a beach and began to drink sea water to exhaustion, but his thirst never calmed. That man was you. All those who are like you go around the world showing their thirst for more and more without ever thinking of others, wallowing in the mire of their misfortune. They think they are rich but they are poor and miserable. Then the head roared:

—Is there anything else you want to say before the feast we've prepared you for?

—Yes! Said Jacob—, who wants to try my flesh first?

—I will! —Replied the selfish without hesitation.

—Come! —So, saying, when the Giant approached, brandishing Orok's sword he cut off his head with one blow. The tottering giant approached bathed in his own blood. Again, Jacob asks:

—Who wants to taste my heart?

—I will—! Said the cruel helplessly.

—Get closer! Jacob exclaimed this time without any fear. —In doing so again the sword whistled through the air and the Giant's second head rolled over to touch his feet, then spoke again.

—Only you remain, and if you want to satisfy your hunger with my body will have to come to me now!

What remains of the Giant's body is bathed in blood, staggering about and again; with a flash the sword makes half circle in the air and the insatiable one's head rolls on the floor, joining the other two. He threads all three heads in the sword, taking them to the entrance of the cave. The animals fall to the floor invaded by fear. The walrus tusk is the first to speak:

—From now on we'll serve as part of your army. You only have to call us with this horn and we'll come to your aid. We are many, as many as the Assassins and we can beat them if you're in command. You delivered us from the giant oppressing us and are willing to pay you back. —Saying this, lowered his head and dropped to the ground a white horn carved with strange symbols; Jacob comes to where his friends are and called them:

—The danger of the giant is gone, come and join me again! Our army is waxed gross; I can call it playing a white horn the Monsters gave me. They'll come to our aid when needed.

○○○

He blows the horn and the first to appear are the fairies, emerging from underneath Orok's cape, the others follow them. The Monsters recovered their stone appearance mimicking the environment and their vast bodies are disguised as ancient rocks covered with moss, fungus and mould. The fairies will light the way down the mountain, but dangers lurk.

Once everybody enters the cave, on the sides they can see huge stone statues that seem to come alive with the lantern's light. The first to talk is a snake that wraps itself around a stone pillar, one of which supports the roof of the cavern. A loud voice is heard when it speaks:

—I'm the advisor for the insecure, for my sake many wars were fought. In ancient times there was one which shook the world. Say my name and that of the war and I'll let you pass...

You're the jealous one, there're many humans whom you bit and women who use you as one of their favourite defects or tricks. You're a loaded gun with a dangerous trap ready to go off too easily. You hurt a lot with your forked tongue and your intrigues. You'll never find peace, as one of your jobs is to sow discord in those who don't understand love. You're corrupted from the beginning of your existence and nobody can trust you. The walls of Troy fell because of you and Cain was your invention. The serpent uncoils slowly from the column, placing dangerously close its ugly head a foot away from him; when it speaks, a foul breath impregnates Jacob face.

—Why do you complain? I'm needed! Don't you realize that if you hadn't betrayed Crystal the way you did you wouldn't feel my presence eating your heart and guts?

—She'd never do such a thing...

—Don't be so sure, every human being has an Achilles' heel, especially when love or sex are involved...—With those words Jacob feels the serpent's bite and for an instant grows jealous. —Does that excuse your foul play? —The serpent asks again with a mocking smile.

—No, it doesn't. I'm purging my fault for having cheated on her and as a conscience I lost her, certainly didn't deserve her. Now I'm looking for my destiny; along my way I discovered I have to be rigorously honest with myself and with others in order to clean my past and get rid of guilt, avoiding problems in the future. I don't know if I'll accomplish all of that, but I have no alternative... I won't lose anything trying.

—I can feel someone else is helping you...

—Yes, his name is Miel.

—Ah! Against him I can't do much, is part of the army that defeated me millennia ago—. Without thinking twice, in one blow Jacob cuts off the snake's head, thus falling to the ground, its body wallowing in painful convulsions. The head speaks again with rage:

—You can't destroy me. I'm more powerful than you'll ever be! I'll soon grow another head, but you'll not be here to see it. This time it'll be ready to inflict even more pain with its forked tongue... Many humans will kill each other because of me!

The party continues its way down, a few steps further, a statue on the other side, with a mirror in its hand, resembling a caryatid speaks with a seductive voice:

—I'm the beautiful one. You can have me in your party and free me from my spell, only say my name and that'll be enough to break it.

—You've many names. You're the smug, immodest, ostentatious, conceited, petulant and arrogant. Your mirror has reflected all the women who were born but certainly none matches your beauty. You're the fruit of pride and love your wealth far too much.

—You're right, but still you haven't told the name by which I'm known. I challenge you to do it. Say my name!

—You're the vain, you have no limits. Soon you'll lose what remains of your beauty and won't look in a mirror again.

—Liar! —She said angrily. —'My beauty will never disappear!

Then, the Stone Woman comes to life, looks in the mirror being amazed with the beauty of a gold mask covering her face, her crimson lips, forming a rictus with provocative smile.

Suddenly the mask falls. And an ugly face, marked by scars and holes left by disease appears when she smiles, revealing a single tooth. Then the woman begins to mourn inconsolably; between sobs she asks:

—Who do you think I truly am?

—I told you, you're the vain, never humbly to accept the beauty you were born with. You wanted to humiliate others and lay your whims over men. You were prey to pride, but... don't cry, you'll be forgiven if you humble yourself and break the mirror in your hand. It shows only vain glories and that flesh is perishable. Old age brings on wrinkles but youth is always in the soul.

At that time the woman breaks the mirror on the floor; the rest of the stone is cracked to pieces just like an egg shell covering her body, she emerges smiling and grateful to be released from her long millennium confinement.

She can't see herself now and she doesn't know what she's become what it once was when being young: one of the most beautiful that was ever born.

—Thanks,' replied with a sigh, I feel light and my beauty does not matter anymore. I know accept gratefully new wrinkles and I'll keep my heart young.

The march continues. In a dark corner hiding his shame, a man bent groaning in the shadows. No one knows his name or why he is there. He rests one arm on the floor, his eyes fixed on a water puddle. When approaching, he implores for mercy.

—Say my name, I must hear it from someone other than me.

—You're Narcissus. The one seduced by your own beauty and never reached the object of your passion. A beautiful and poisonous flower grows on graves, carrying your name. You're a child of selfishness and vanity.

—Would you like to free me from this painful position? —Narcissus asks distressed. —My back hurts and I'm sick of myself. Maybe I could get to be part of your entourage, I think I've learned the lesson that you gave the vain, my own mother. From her I inherited my faults…

—And also, her virtues! I can do it only if you promise not to look for yourself in water's pools, avoiding mirrors at all times. If you forget your promise, you'll return to your old self. — At that time Narcissus cries with joy, exclaiming loud:

—I'm the most beautiful, I'm back to being free! —But as soon as he shouts that, it becomes a hunchbacked old stone in the same position he was at the beginning. So, Jacob says with dismay.

—You lost this opportunity. Now you'll have to wait until the day Miel's eyes passes by here, meanwhile, meditate and recognize what attracted your misfortune.

Before entering the circular room, they find the last of the stone statues along the cave's corridor. Its tall, covered with a tunic reaching the ground. It has a long beard and a hood covering his head. A stone owl stands on its left shoulder; its right hand carries a pitchfork and the left a book. It speaks in a tremulous voice:

—Say my name otherwise you'll become an insignificant hungry bird.

—I love birds. Many accompany me. I wouldn't mind

to be changed into one of them. Also know your name and why you turned into a stone. You're Merlin, one of the greatest magicians ever existed, but you met someone more powerful than you and she was Morgana the deadliest sorceress. You fell under her charm and she under yours. She and you both are evil monsters and must remain attached to the rock forever.

—Do you know what the book I hold in my hand is?

—Yes! *"The Acromanto"* —, he answered cautiously, —one of spells and incantations. In it are listed all the secrets of magic. It's best to stay turned to stone. There is taught the secret of the "philosophical stone", which it has the power to turn into gold everything it touches. Humanity is already unhinged in the blind pursuit of money. If someone discovered how to turn everything into gold, man would die of hunger—. At that time the owl comes to life, before flying it says.

—See you soon. You overcame Merlin with your wisdom but not me. I'm ready to keep fighting against you, you didn't recognize me, and I'm the one who watches you every night. I still have enough time…

MIEL

Santiago Martinez Concha

VIII

Soon the party reached the circular room where the three-headed giant dwelt. They observed several closed doors and on each of them a sign. Moon and Sun speak with worried faces.

—You'll have to open them all and at the end you'll discover who you're, otherwise you'll never reach your destination to the place where the coffer with life's secret hides. The last door will take you to a place where you can hear laughter and rest until dawn. You'll be surprised with them more than you think. —The first door is marked with a sign up that says:

"I'm what I'm because of who I was,
I'll be what I'll be because of who I am."

Jacob opens the door and in the darkness a voice speaks with a laugh. This time however much your wisdom is you can't answer me. Who am I? What you read is... true or false? —Jacob answers without hesitation:

—You're the liar one. All fooling with your lies is tricked; therefore, what is written is partly true and partly false. If you don't change, what is written there is true, but if you change it and you agree to the truth is false. The secret is to want to change.

—I can't, said the liar. I have always lied. Want to see me?

—Yes, so I can avoid you in the future. —He calls for

the light and the room lights, but sees no one, however hears the voice again:

—I can come and go at will. I'm the master of disguise, I can make the truth be confused with lies and light with darkness. —The words came like javelins to his mind. "Remember, things are not what they seem to be". Without hesitation he ordered the light to disappear. Then he asked the fairies for Orok's cape. The site remains in the dark. When light is back, the liar asks intrigued:

—Where are you? I can't see you.

—That's the truth. I can also come and go at will without having to lie. By accepting you can't see me, you told the truth and accept that you always lied also did. Never again you'll be the same. Once you know the truth and accept it, you'll never let go of it. Then he jumped out from under the cape, crosses the threshold and closed the door tightly. A voice cries and furious blows are heard from within.

—I was cheated!

—¡No, I beat you with the truth!

Then he turns to the second door, where he can read above a mysterious sentence making him feel very uneasy.

"I once had a treasure and lost it in a desert.
It was a long night and I lost all my might."

Jacob opens the door and again this room is dark, he hears a man's cry in the background pleading with trembling voice:

—Leave me alone, don't look at my sadness If you tell me who I'm you can help me to recover my treasure, otherwise it's best for you to leave now.

—I know who you're and what you want. You're the infidel, one who lost the treasure of faith. The desert is the way and the nights are long of all who seek or have that treasure. Don't miss the light of hope. During the dark hours of life sometimes faith is lost. It becomes necessary for you retrace your paces to find it. You're still alive! Come, join me if you want, leave your confinement with the remaining breath you have and dry your tears. At the end is the reward. Perhaps you'll find it and the chest that guards it. The man stands up and says with gratitude's tears:

—Thank you, your words of encouragement help me and comforts me. I'll be on my knees every night until I find it. — Next door is the widest and remains wide open, the room is illuminated with a dimmed light and above the door entrance is written:

"Here begins the fate of those who lost their way.
Here ends the way of those who lost their fate."

A sweet smell of oriental incense fills the air. On a highly polished ebony table, a huge golden apple surrounded by drinks and elixirs of all colours and sorts can be seen. At the back, a sleepy—eyed beautiful woman wrapped in red silk, lying on a bed of gold—coated fabrics and cushions covered in exquisite silk brocades. She is barefoot. Her arms are covered with rings of gold and silver as well as her ankles; fingers, hands and feet are decorated with platinum rings inscribed with ancient runes and jewels embedded in them. Her breasts are covered with fine gold necklaces decorated with vulture's figures spreading its wings casted in black, red and blue cobalt glazes. From her ears hung large pearls and a turban wraps her head. The woman is smoking a water pipe and the bubbles' sound, like a purr within the glass bottle, comes every time she sucks the pipe's air that helps her cool her lungs. Her sleepy voice breaks the silence:

—I've been expecting you... Just say my name and you can stay as long as you want. On the table you'll find elixirs to help you sharing my delights. Come to my side. Your appetite is known to me and your mouldy heart reminds my own. Remember

Dalila? I also know hers—... under the beautiful woman's turban, poisonous snakes come out, sliding down across her body and her beauty becomes purulent showing a face marked by scars. He answers her humiliated.

—You're the lustful one, I know both sides of your coin. On one hand the pleasure and the other the pain of what you offer. You can no longer conquer me. I've experienced the void left after being with you. Your messy appetite wearies all those who proved your treacherous elixirs and delights; because of you, more than a king or popes fell to the depths. The list of men and women you seduced is longer than the greatest of hosts.

Hastily he went out of that place, closing the door behind him and in doing so noted that the lock has a key placed in the keyhole. He makes two turns, leaving the woman in the middle of a laugh giving him goose bumps. Then he goes to the next door. Once it opens it, looks back into a dark room. Not knowing what to expect calls to light to illuminate a written sign above the entrance where he can read in blood red letters:

"What I kept I lost. What I had I never gave.
What I gave I never felt, I only thought of me."

In the background he can see the body of a man tied with a rope hanging from a foot, like the one featured in the Tarot cards showed him by Sahay. Below are some of the man's gold coins scattered on the floor, then he begs pitifully.

—Say my name. Maybe the one guiding your way, when he comes back will have mercy on me and set me free. I purged my sin after having been suspended from this rope for many years.

—You're the stingy one; the coins on the ground are those which fell from your pockets and didn't give to the poor. ¿Do you remember blessing with long prayers at your table thanking God for the bread and delicacies you'd eat, thinking that was all? However, you never played your part to help satisfy the bellies of the poor. You're a hypocrite! If you'd shared at least a shred of the leftovers from your table with the poor, God would've appreciated it. In your vault is all that you won and could not share with anyone. You took over your family's goods to increase your wealth, but ever returned a penny or made repairs of all you stole. You're like a devious octopus, false, stubborn, envious and contemptible. Those are your tentacles that suck the blood of those who served you and never returned the favour to the same extent. Every time you borrowed a widow's savings to increase your fortune, never returned anything to her or to her children. You do merits and close your eyes when you walk into a church for all to admire your devotion, but in your heart, you keep your treasures locked and your mind counts to the last penny. ¡I hope you'll hang in there until the time comes and the rope that holds your upside-down rots, letting fall into to the depths you deserve!

Closing that door, he goes to the next. A sign above the threshold light shines in the dim light of lanterns held by fairies and says so:

"We are three who ate of the bitter fruits along the path.
We are three who drank, finding no peace in our heart."

When he calls the light, shows three women's bodies tied with thick ropes to a pole, each bearing on its shoulders an animal's head. The first shows a tiger, the second a coyote and a third a pig. Then, a roaring tiger asks:

—Who am I?

—You're the passionate one. You suffer from a disease difficult to cure. You're violent and lose control of yourself easily. You have caused many wars and family disputes and because of you many crimes are committed. Then the tiger's head gives a terrifying roar and questions again.

—Can you help me? What should I do to get rid of this disease I have and with which I myself have been the hardest hit? I thought at some point that with it I could conquer anything.

—The first thing you've done is to recognize you suffer from it. Now you must descend from the pedestal of pride and step on your own ego whenever you can.

Again, the group hears an even longer roar; the woman's body with a tiger's head is released from her bonds and becomes a prehistoric young woman of great beauty covered in animal skins. She addresses the group speaking with her heart:

—My name before I became a tiger was Ajana, which means *"problem"* but now that I've been released, Miel has changed it in an instant by that of Ajiela which means *"God's sister"*. I was once a powerful princess in a prehistoric tribe. I was also stubborn and sacrificed it all for not listening to the elder's viewpoints. While in a meeting with my husband and the tribe's, shamans, some of them contradicted me for just cause. I, without hesitation ordered him to a deep cave and stayed there all abandoned ever since. His advice would have prevented an atrocious war against my neighbours. If I had heard him, I would still have a husband and our children by my side. He was chained by one who conquered our tribe; our children scattered or abandoned and never heard from them. I moored here since because of my ego and for not listening to all that opposed my stubbornness and capricious designs. Obstinacy blinds whoever the sufferer. Now, if I as a token of gratitude I would like to follow you, serving up as the humblest cone of your companions, asking Miel to let me release my shackled husband. —At that moment a poor and ragged man fur covered appears at her side answering:

—My name is Vivar. I forgive you for locking me up without listening to my advice. I know how you can recover me

and your children. When the time comes, you'll have us with you.
—Then the jackal's head spoke in a voice where they perceived his craftiness:

—Tell me who I'm and I'll tell you who you're...

—You have two facets. You're the envious and the gossiper one, always wanting to do or have what others do, are or earned, usually without success. You're never satisfied with yourself. Like sow doubt and discord. For your sake many were killed, chained, betrayed and lost their prestige due to your gossip and slander. Deep pity you, you hide low self-esteem, you're miserable, false, treacherous and ugly. You're a double—edged knife, spread with snake venom. Your illness is incurable and so are your vile dark purposes. I don't want to be your friend and you better stay away from you. Now answer me, who do you say I'm?

—You're the one I envy, Jacob, the swallows' tamer, who is searching for his destiny. If you don't find it, I'll be waiting on this site, but if you do, will envy you even more, because your destiny isn't only one but two...

—Two? Did you say I have two destinations? He asked out of curiosity.

—That's right... Two destinations! Sometimes things are not what they seem. At the end you'll understand, in the meantime I'll think of your words and try to change... Perhaps one-day Miel will release me from my chains...

Then it's the turn of the pig-headed woman, asking in a mixture between laziness and boredom...

—Who am I?

—You represent the glutton and the addict; you wallow in the mud and eat garbage. Once a rich man threw pearls, but in the place where you eat don't distinguish what you swallow. You represent all addictions that exist.

—Tell me, do you think you could help me? I'm sick of the dirt around me.

—Would you be willing to be rigorously honest and go

to any lengths to get your freedom?

Yes, yes, I believe, that is what I desire most.

At that moment Miel comes and frees her from the ropes that tie her to the pole.

—So, you're free! All you had to do was to recognize and accept your illness. From now on you'll be yourself again—. Instantly, the body and the pig's head turn into another beautiful woman wearing a long braid in the fashion of the Amazons of old. She nobly and bravely, draws a sword and answers:

—I must undo the wrong I did. My name is Nova and thousands of men and women fell into my net carrying with them behind this terrible flaw that they learned from me when I took the wrong road, now I must go back and repair the evil I've done. I can't join you yet, because before I ought to release from its chains many for the many wrongs I did—. Then vanished in a swirl until it disappears completely.

A little further, he expected a whisper echoes composed of thousands of sounds. A large room decorated in the background with a red glare and gallant array is illuminated by the fire of a huge fireplace. Pictures of old big shots showing her erect and martial moustaches bear witness that there ran with irreverent gesture time and oblivion, claiming lives and turning things pale. He recognizes there many of his own ancestors, which he once saw in his father's old photo album, kept somewhere in the cart. The pictures make him smile and laugh. Thought how he would look in a few years. Suddenly hundreds of laughs invade the premises, including one he recognizes and sounds familiar and asked surprised:

—You look familiar. ¿Do I know you?

—Of course, you do, after many years today you recovered your own laugh. I'm you! You forgot to laugh along the way many years ago. Now you can laugh at yourself. All the laughter you hear is yours. Every time you laugh, you break one link of the chain you built around yourself. You locked yourself in a stone tower on the day your father died. At that time, you felt badly hurt and decided not to feel anything ever since, ignoring all your feelings, but now every time you recognize them, you'll feel lighter. From now on we'll always be with you.

The going gets harder, this time the road is steep and a storm soon envelops everything. Thunderbolts fell everywhere. Torrential rain moves off huge rocks and what were dangerous streams become rivers that roll down the mountain threatening to anyone who wants to cross them. As they advance, the silhouette of a huge palace crowning a village surrounded by a wall and lost in the distance can be seen through the mist. Moon and Sun tell with joy. —We found it! We must get to it and take shelter before the storm gets worst. No one lives there now; centuries ago, the inhabitants were killed by the mercenaries. In its dungeons you can still see the bodies of those who were tortured. Other legends tell that in its basements are many of those left alive and were turned to stone over the centuries expecting to be redeemed —. Jacob, as if he were another very different from the one only five days ago, speaks with enthusiasm:

—After the tests I went through I endured, I lost my fear. I think it's best to get there and wait for the storm to subside.

MIEL   Santiago Martinez Concha

IX

The palace is located on the tip of a mountain that is born as a lonely island in the middle of a lake full of unknown dangers. A lonely and abandoned town surrounded by a stone wall, connected with a bridge leading to a square and from there, a steep street goes through the village getting to the palace gates. His ghostly silhouette lights from afar with rays born in the eye of the storm and its tallest towers resemble spears piercing dark clouds. The town and palace are attached to the mountain with seven bridges forming a stone lace overlay and are the only accesses that connect to them.

Sun and Moon explain to Jacob why since immemorial time the site is known as the 'Seven Winds Palace'. The mountain wind to pass through the arcades' lace and the seven towers, produced the name of the king and queen who once inhabited there. The three higher bridges connected the town with some of the most important secret places. The first, guarded by two dragons led into a square, the town and the palace. The second guarded by two fairies, led to the underground rooms and to the queens secrete chamber. The third guarded by two princes led to a princess' secret chamber. The fourth guarded by two servants, ran into the great hall where feasts happened and the round polished oracle's table still exists. The fifth guarded by two bears, led to the grain and food warehouses. The sixth defended by two huge lions served as a road which allowed the army and war machines to move through.

On the seventh and final with two warriors guarding it, circulated the prisoners taken in battles to their final destination in the castle's dungeons. But none of the guards were now there. All died or fled the day the mercenaries attacked the seven bridges, the subjects were taken prisoners and stole the queen and her daughter the princess, the most beautiful princess who ever lived. —Then Jacob adds hopefully:

—We can go in there; no one will stop us. The dragons guarding the first bridge we have to cross have died.

—Don't be so sure, responded Sun and Moon. One died but the other escaped, and nobody knows where it is. They say once trained, they are like dogs, being loyal to their masters even if it costs them their lives. Never lose them, and if they do, they'll seek until they find them. —The road is getting narrower; soon reaches the highest place, where they can see the first bridge. It's flanked on either side by two stone giants each armed with a huge sword.

—Those giants were once alive, —says Gen, —but the mercenaries turned them into stones. They forced them to say the magic words:

"Mut-A-Me-Met-A-Mu
You're me and I'm you."

If you want to break the spell, open the book with the Big Tree embedded in its paste and ask it how to undo the curse. He carries the book inside his bag, takes it in his hands and shouts out loud:

"Lumen Arboris!"

The engraving on the pasta with the Big Tree's image

lights with rivers of fire; he opens the book and two words begin to write by themselves as if with an invisible magic hand, in a blood's coloured ink:

"Umatem Ematum!"

Facing the two giants Jacob utters the two magic words and opens his eyes wide with disbelief; the huge creatures start coming to life after waking from their slumber.

—What were the words you spoke? Balm asks surprised.

—They are the reverse of the spell.

—Who needs our help? The colossus standing on the left asks.

—¡I, Jacob! I'm searching for my destiny!

—What is your name? —Ask the fairies addressing the colossus.

—Mastodon and he is my twin brother Margedon. We belong to the one who awoke us.

—The fairies respond surprising him:

—Don't you remember us? We are April and May, the spring's fairies, we're identical sisters, the water' daughters and the caretakers of the bridge below.

—Oh Yes! I remember you now... it was so long ago... that terrible day when everything happened. We'll be serving the one so called Jacob, the Swallows' Tamer, by the time he needs us.

The party begins to cross the bridge and when in the middle, Balm screams in horror.

—Someone is coming, is a huge dragon and I can see its silhouette far away in the distance!

The silhouette approaches in a rapid descent to where the group is gathered. Sun and Moon hand in hand vacuum slide and plunge to their deaths hundreds of feet below, against the cold waters of the lake. You can then see the silhouette of the dragon against moon and three people traveling on his back. They're Orok and his family. The dragon squeezes dangerously through the arches that make up the fifth stone lace bridge, take in its clutches the two lovers before they crash into the icy waters of the lake and place them safely, in front the wall's stone gates that give access to the town. The procession crosses the bridge and all are glad to see each safe. Orok speaks first and politely receives them:

—Welcome to my palace, or what remains of it. Morg looked up for me until it found me. From the air we saw a huge crowd approaching in the distance. They are the mercenaries. They learned when they saw Morg and us on his back of our return. Their dark forces want to destroy us again. Surely, we'll all die if we don't hide away from here.

—¡No, this time we'll fight! Our army is bigger than you think. —Jacob exclaims with confidence. Takes the white horn from his back and blows it with all his might… a long, deep sound, as if from the bowels of the earth, booms with echoes that can be heard everywhere. It's so powerful that the Assassins can also hear it and look at each other in bewilderment, but that does not stop them in their march. When sound reaches the place where the Monsters are converted into huge stones, hear the echoes windblown and awaken. True to their promise, are in support of the call. An infernal dust rises from the ground with the progress of this new army. These animals are huge, willing to take revenge for the entire Assassins' wrongs they caused in the past. Soon the two armies along different paths arrive at the site under the eye of the storm, but still can't see each other yet.

Orok plans the defensive strategy. Morg is sent to persuade the Monsters to hide in the rear, allowing the Assassins' troops to reach the bridge. At a horn signal must attack from the rear pushing them over the cliff where cold waters of the lake with unknown dangers await them. Morg goes back across the bridge and is placed in front. Behind are the giants, Orok and Jacob in the middle and prepared for battle. The rest of the party remains behind. It soon becomes the most ferocious of history's battles. The bridge is narrow and not easy to cross. In the midst of combat Jacob, plays the horn again and the Monsters attack the Assassins from the rear. But something unexpected happens. Thousands of birds guided by huge golden eagles are released to attack from the top of the castles' higher towers. Swallows in flocks like the swarm of a hive, attack the Assassins who are on the bridge, pecking them everywhere they can, while the great eagles help push them to the vacuum. Those who can make it to the other bridge's head where Morg, the giants, Orok and Jacob are, don't roll with better luck. The flames spewing from Morg's jaws begin to fry the Assassins. Those who manage to escape meet the powerful colossi's force which throws them to the vacuum against the cliff's rocks and the icy waters of the lake below. Meanwhile, Orok threaded with his lance the Assassins who approach him and Jacob using his sword cuts some heads and guts as well. When the Assassins play withdrawal is too late for them. All perish with the strategy developed by Orok.

The entrance to the town square is as triumphant one. Morg enters firs followed later by the giants, Orok, Jacob and the rest of the party. The town seems deserted and vines have invaded it everywhere. A shrill voice and the beating of a metal spoon against a pan can be heard somewhere.

—Who's there? Questions Orok amazed.

—I, Serafina. For a thousand years I've beaten this cauldron where I prepared my delicious tortillas' eggs that were once the delight of my king and lord, but I have no man of taste to try them now, all are gone and I'm the only one left.

—I'm Orok, your king and this time I'm back to stay. Where are the others? —Serafina prostrates with outstretched arms and cries.

—Welcome, my king and lord! I knew you'd come

back! I was the only one who was not tortured or turned to stone. The Assassins loved my tortillas and had no one else who could prepare them for that reason they let me live. The only way to break the spells of those you asked for is to pronounce the words found in the Book of Life or the Big Book as others call it.

Jacob taking the book in his hands exclaims. *"Lumen Arboris!"* Rivers of fire again run the tree, he opens it and questions:

—Where are the town's people? —Thousands of names begin to appear in the book, written with dark red blood ink. Again he asks:

—What should we do now?

The book answers:

"Meditate!
Open your minds!
Open your hearts!
Be willing to try!
In honesty and discipline,
There is freedom.
That is the golden key!"

When they open their eyes after meditating what the book taught them, hundreds of people missing after the first battle with the Assassins centuries ago, gather to greet Orok and his entourage. April and May fairies begin to fly around touching what they find and the vines are removed, giving way to all kinds of flowers and spring greenery. When they reach the castle's top, crossing a bridge over a deep ditch they finally arrive to the place where the oracle's table is. Jacob looks out a window; in the distance one can see a snow—capped volcano halfway. Something else catches his eye. He sees at the bottom of the lake something emitting bright light flashes traversing the crystal-clear waters and reaching the surface. Huge prehistoric fish with sharp teeth, capable of swallowing a human being than a mouthful dwell in the background. Orok and the fairies are watching him in silence. What he must do, must do it alone.

This time his destination is near and it still depends on many others. As in the past he must look for the group's support. Nothing would've been achieved without their help. They go out to the town's plaza, the dragon, docile as a dog, bend its legs, and in a half jump, Jacob places himself on its back. Morg will take him to a lake shore, where there's a boat with two oars. The animal takes flight in circles around the mountain and the castle. The view of Orok's hidden realm is magnificent from that point, then Morg rapidly descends towards the boat, but he ignores a great danger that waits. When they reach the beach, the dragon rests lightly on the sand, Jacob gets down from its back and the dragon says:

—That's Acheron's boat, the ferryman of death. Others call him Miel, love's messenger. Don't get in it if your intentions are not totally honest and pure, you may never return.

Morg takes flight and returns to the palace, leaving him alone with his thoughts. Jacob pushes the boat, sliding in the water, leaving behind soundless waves, climbs into it and begins to row vigorously to the point where he saw the light from above. When he arrives, jumps into the water and the cold make him feel a strange tingling sensation. In an instant his past is gone; his wounds are closed and hope reborn. He knows he's finally discovered the coffer with life's origins. Gathering all his strength, he dives, down as he's able to kept the air in his lungs. There in the background he sees the coffer. Tries to get to it but he can't, the coffer appears to be in a deeper place than he thought. Returns to the surface and sees the fairies resting on the water's surface, watching him, repeating at the same time:

—You can't bring it with you if your intentions aren't pure! An evil woman opened it long time ago, sprouting from it all the evil that exists. Before she found it, the coffer was lying at the bottom of the lake for thousands of years, from the time life began on Earth. Hidden in it it's also the secret of life and all the music notes that exist. She only let out the bad, but the good things are still there waiting for someone to rescue them. The price is high, even your own life; so, think about it, but in return you'll make many people happy. Some people have the gift to sing and understand all the music, Crystal is one of them; you're the other with your whistling. She is your soul mate. Learn to value her.

The first time you both heard the music was in the rain. Over time you learned to listen it everywhere, since then you both loved the music that reminded you of the origin of music. You both each have your own way. She can sing like sirens and charm all who to listen to her. You on the other hand, whistle like the birds and sing like the poets. Remember, you found your soul mate, but you'll lose her, like your gifts, if you ignore your feelings or hers. Feelings are the only thing that connects us to our own reality, if you don't express them, the other person will never know where you stand, and you'll grow apart and end up alone.

Jacob asked the fairies permission to take the coffer from the lake bottom and they answer that this time he'll have to load it on his back. He takes a deep breath, dives again, to note that this time he goes down faster than before. The bottom where he thought he saw the coffer turns out to be just an illusion. Feels when something breaks, then falls flat on a white sand dune and next sees it. He's under a water dome and the bellies of big fish with sharp teeth can be seen above his head. The chest is a box of solid gold glittering with a lid on which a tree styled in the same way as in the book's cover he carries with him. Try to lift the cap but can't, take a deep breath and exclaims. *"Lumen Arboris!"* Next the box is marked with rivers of fire showing all arabesques and carvings. The lid opens by itself and two interlocking spirals such as streamers, formed by thousands of small creatures like fireflies flying escape light, illuminated the cave. A wonderful singing voice of a woman in which he recognized Crystal's, wrap every corner. It says:

"Run, run, now I can see!
If you come to the top,
you'll hear me sing,
if you try to reach me,
I'll have to hide,
search, search, in the depths
of your being, only then you can see me,
I'm your soul mate, I'll be your wife.
If you love me, but you'll have to wait,
you still need to learn not to ignore me:
that is learning to love. You're still not done,
so, you must seek, trust and accept,
and have the courage to dream,
with yesterday, today and tomorrow.
Run, run, I'll have to wait.
Soon you'll see a place
with fear, sadness and tears.
At the end of the road you'll hear its cry
it's the wind crossing a lonely park
Then hear it say:
Everything is gone and is not coming back.
Be patient and learn how to stay.
When the great eagle, teaches you to fly,
then you'll see, Earth's skin,
in pain with cries of birth, defeated,
ill, without water and nothing to give,
so without fear, begin to scream:
It's time, time to love again!
to save the land, the seas and the air!
Run, run, and take a deep breath,

*I need to be loved
and then to be saved."*

The luminous beings are soon reunited above the gold chest and enter into it. The lid is closed. When attempting to lift the chest, this time it feels lighter and can be done without effort, then opens the book and asks worried:

—Now what should I do? I know I can't exit reaching the vaulted ceiling to find my way up to the surface...

Soon some words form with ink and blood that read:

*"Use the instrument with the needle of life.
Follow its course and find the light."*

He removes the instrument from his neck and orders it with fearless voice:

— Show me the exit!

The wheels began to turn in various directions making noises similar to a clock mechanism and the larger needle stops and lit bookmarking. With the box on his back he begins to follow the intricacies of the cave indicated by the instrument. He arrives to a place where there is a spiral staircase and begins to ascend. He soon realizes that he is in the centre of the mountain below the castle. After a long climb reaches the oracle's room where they are all waiting. He then places the coffer on the black stone table. Using the hole in the roof, the same where the star lights reflected its path on the polished surface of the black table, a huge golden eagle comes down flying in circles into the great hall. Then the eagle asks in an intriguing tone:

— Do you know how to fly?

—No... I don't have wings like you do!

—You're wrong, you have them! It's only a matter of

imagine them. ¿Do you remember as a child when asleep, and you imagined you were flying? Actually, you did fly. Every human being can do it as a child, but then, with the passing of life, the burden becomes heavier and grownups forget about it. Your spirit first and then the flesh. Would you like to try again? It's required if you want to get to the top of the volcano covered halfway with snow. Nobody has ever been there. Close your eyes and follow my words... Now fly!

He rose through the air and out the hole in the roof. He was flying alone, recalled how as a child could do the same. Through the roof of the house of his parents, went flying over the city and a neighbouring a mountain forest.

Sometimes he felt the vertigo produced by the height and others found it difficult to stay on the right course. The great golden eagle watched his movements this time by his side. Below, he saw the lake and the castle seemed distant. An immense volcano seemed to be getting closer. He started flying in circles above the volcano's mouth and then landed on its top. Suddenly he heard his father's voice filled with emotion:

—It's an extinct volcano covered with snow halfway, as the first letter of your name. You'll soon hear Crystal singing but you'll not see her. Her voice is pristine as snow crystals. In the mountain there is another boat, when you get there look for a hatch, open it and go inside. That boat was the big egg shell which contained the germ of the new creation. It housed all life without having to walk the long road that led there. You have been chosen to build one that will save the seed of life within the earth.

From the top he could see the earth around the volcano and he saw a boat covered with snow, next to a deep crack on the ice. They had flown up there with great difficulty almost dying of cold. Once they reached the immense structure the great eagle said persuasively:

— You must go in alone; it has waited for you for centuries. This place is a sanctuary; I'll watch for intruders. Millennia ago, the boat was at the top of the volcano, but with each melt came down a little more from the place where it originally was. Many intrepid men have tried get here, but none have succeeded. They all forgot how to fly! Some died in the attempt and others were lost or swallowed by the huge crack in the ice never to be seen again.

He then saw a hatch on top of the deck, lifted the frozen lid and went inside.

Crystal's crystal voice could be heard accompanying him. It was dark and after thousands of years, he felt the scent of wood from which the boat was made. Menacing icicles as sharp swords hung from the ceiling and occasionally fell to the ground making loud sounds. The dim light coming through the hatch showed hundreds of compartments that were lost in the distance. It was Noah's ark. Then he knew that his mission was to rescue what was left of life in spirals and seed banks and preserve all again in the deepest snow of any of the poles. In his dream he also descended into the volcano through its dark mouth. At the bottom there was a huge circular space where dozens of tunnels came connecting with the hidden world of the buried cities. Small creatures with big eyes and long arms lived there. In the centre of that space had a smaller mouth seemed to go into the centre of the earth, out of it came smoke and blue flames. He knew he should not go there. He then heard Miel's voice in a warning tone:

—There only go those for which there is no return. If you enter you must bear witness to what awaits those who didn't fulfil the most sacred of duties and sinned against love in the extreme. If you don't enter, you must do the same. Henceforth the real will mix with the unreal, the true with the false, but you'll know how to differentiate it, because you'll be seeing only with the eyes of spirit.

At dawn he woke up with fear and with the 'chest of

life' locked in his memory. He must make an urgent call for nations to save what they can from the world heritage, keeping the spiral of life, in airtight containers, in the depths of a mountain or the poles. Crimes against nature had already reached the ninth circle of heavens. In descending order, the entire food chain of the Earth was in danger. Thousands of species were to become extinct on the surface in the air and in the sea. He saw from the air devastated huge tracts of forest, deserts advancing like a cancer on the skin of the earth, about to devour it. Clouds of dust enveloped it everywhere. The smoke rising from factories could be seen from afar and huge chimneys seemed headlights of death. Dumps and scrap fields rose like barren mountains. Everything was orchestrated by the evil of greed, the same as ever. Soon everything would be made again. Man should either change or be exterminated.

While writing about all this, an owl watches him from outside with malice. Thinks it's won the battle. That the temptation he put on his path will make him loose the course of his destination. But what it doesn't know is that Miel has freed him from the sin committed with Dalila and that he's found the chest with the secret of life.

Santiago Martinez Concha

X

Jacob went to lecture his students that morning with swollen eyelids and red eyes. At first, he asked them if they knew the origin of the word sign. Nobody knew. He wrote it on the blackboard with white chalk:

Sign:

"Something that represents or replaces another."

Again, he wrote to illustrate them:

"Her sadness seemed a sign of her abandonment,
her love a sign of her commitment,
her beauty a sign of her soul,
her soul a sign of her purity,
her joy a sign of her hope,
her hope, a sign of her beliefs,
her faith a sign of her confidence,
her life a sign of my life…"

He then explained that signs are visible or invisible and asked them with what kind of a sign they left home that morning and if they had marked or designated themselves in some way. The students were silent, absorbing every word. He continued:

—Sign and design are the same.

His students looked at him surprised, never thought of

178

that. He cleared his desk and asked to them to approach it placing on it all they carried around their necks. They students placed the objects neatly on the wooden surface. Medals, medallions and amulets of all kinds were piled next to each other, as in a domino of spells. Shell necklaces and coloured stones, someone put an iron swastika and another a silver marijuana leaf, a medal with a saint, a cameo, a pearl and a teardrop diamond earring embedded in gold. All were there. When it came Roger's turn, he was pale and didn't move. Jacob asked him with scorn:

—What's happening with you, perhaps you have nothing…?

—Yes, I have something! —he answered fiercely—, just I don't want to show it to anyone!

—Why are you ashamed? Isn't your sign something that represents you, which also speaks about you?

Then Roger came up and in an act of courage placed his amulet on the table. It was the devil! There was a deep silence for a moment and for the first time Jacob didn't know what to say.

When he got home that night, the first thing he did was to open his desk's drawer, searching for the signs of his own life. He realized that someday after his death someone would come and clean the drawer and would put his life in the trash. Those charitable hands! All they wanted was to see his desk clean and tidy. That person would look at his old photo album and say: ¡there he is, look how young he looked! This photo was taken some years before his death! ¡He left nothing, just a drawer full of old useless things! He lowered his eyes and felt himself invaded by that profound loneliness and fascinating sadness he knew so well. The thought of Crystal ate his entrails.

He looked out the window watching the wall across the street. As in a giant screen, the shadows of the night projected on it phantasmagorical figures. Then he realized that his soul was divided by a wall. On one side was Crystal, his students, the monk, the cloister, the old lady who sold candy in the square's corner, Agnes who painted sunflowers, Sarcasm, José Antonio, the sound of Sunday's bells calling parishioners to attend church, the scream of children playing in the plaza, the smell of roasted corn and the bark of a lonely dog. On the other side was the order given to him by the monk. Without thinking twice took the pen from the drawer where he kept his memories and angrily wrote:

SHAME

"A wall... A long wall... A very long wall...
And then slowly begins to curl
like a snake trying to devour us.
A wall that never ends, that divides us into two at will.
A wall that includes and excludes,
that separates and unite, that guides.
A wall that embraces,
which slowly caresses itself with the sun,
licking with its edge the hills beyond,
A wall that
watches,
guides,
impinges,
waits...
A long wall... Long ... Very long ...
And then slowly begins to curl
like a snake trying to devour us..."

Amidst the shadows of the night, he heard the whistle of the watchman, the howl of a dog and thought again of the wall, a stone wall, a white wall, a mud wall, a wall in silence.

Beyond the wall, the black silhouette of a huge oak loomed against the sky. Standing in the shadows of the tree, an owl was watching him.

He searched desperately at the bottom of the drawer and found a photo of Crystal. He felt his heart open again, blood crying from within and imprisoned the photo against his chest.

That night he was afraid of re—encountering the angel. He was not sure if he wanted to see him again. He opened the door of his room, noticed that everything was in order. After a little washing open the window to let the fresh air invade his lungs and began to meditate. He thought about the masks he was made of and the fact that he would have to remove them all if he wanted to be him. The risk, of course, would be very high. Again, he rose and took his pen, caressed it for a long time like the fingers of his beloved, then, with effort, scrawled on the white of his notebook and some tears fell on his words as a watercolour of his passion. What he wrote relieved his heart and hope returned.

He realized he was alone, lonelier than he ever imagined. No longer would hear Crystal's words. His life at that moment had no north, with the strength he had reread what he had written.

"It is difficult to write ... It must be that I'm changing ... Every time I change the ideas and words escape from me never to return. Every so often there is a metamorphosis in me, my skin falls and I change colours. Sometimes I mimicked with other things around me, others shoulder by contrast, or disappear, I do not want to be found and go to faraway places that nobody understands but me.

When I start to change, I have several symptoms that occur suddenly and never know how or when it will arrive. First starts the pain, a terrible pain to leave behind what I got with so much effort. Gradually things cease to matter; pains go away and I start walking slowly as a child full of fears in an unknown world the surrounds me, in darkness, where the only constants are the good memories of what I experienced in the past. The bad things are forgotten, lost or someone took them and never returned them. Well, sometimes I think it is better to live without the bad things, only with the good ones and that only happens every time I change. The bad things are impregnated in the skin that I drop.

Sometimes the changes are very fast. I sleep with my old skin like crocodiles sleeping in the sun and when I wake up, I don't know who I am or if I'm other which I forgot. Other times change is very slow. I drop scale by scale until naked, then I hide, become vulnerable, everything affects me, it leaves its mark and I bleed easily, covered with scars. That skin I don't like and I already changed it long ago. When naked, I let the wind dry out the raw flesh, until I grow the skin I now have. A skin I'll be leaving hopefully for a better one, one that I'll change again, time over time and that is the risk of change. I never know what I'll be next."

Amid the shadows of his room he smelled, impregnated in the sheets Crystal's roses' perfume. He thought if she had been there, but it was all a delusion. She was gone from his life forever. How many times had he made love to her he past? She chose from the beginning, the window's side. She liked to wake up feeling the sun caressing her skin; he preferred the right side. She snuggled against his body like a snail in a shell. Their love dance was perfected over time. But now he was alone and began experiencing the empty nest syndrome. He realized that the greatest pain comes from the soul and that there is no growth without change, no change without pain. The only way to reach his destiny was to change. He them turned to writing:

"The risk of change is the biggest challenge a human being may face. If we fail to love, we fail to life. If we fail to be happy, we fail to love. The torrent of our tears is part of God's tears. God is within us. When we met our goal of loving we die to be renewed in love, that's why love never ends and always renews itself."

That same night he had another dream...

This time a being not as tall as Miel but equally beautiful presented by the side of his bed. He was empty handed and he had wings that seemed too large for his body size. His eyes were the same colour as Crystal's. Heard his words as a soft whisper when he made him a proposal:

—Want to know your Mask of Fear? If you do, you should travel with me. You can return in the way of life to those dark places where fear and pain hide. Everything ultimately comes down to failures in love. ¿Do you know why you are so sad? ¿Are you ready to heal and be happy? The wounds of the body do not matter; the wounds of the soul are the ones that count. You were created long before you were born. You yourself chose to inhabit the corpse you now have and to live the life you choose. You have to learn from your past mistakes and the sins you committed against love in order to help yourself and others. God waits for you filled with love. We are all part of him. You'll see him when you die.

Jacob listened fascinated, only the monk knew that and could speak so well. He looked at the angel looking for an answer. The idea of happiness was so abstract and distant that it had no place in his life now. Then he asked with uncertainty:

—And Crystal... Can I see her again? ¡I want to love and be happy!

—Almost nothing what you ask! If that's what you want you shall have it, but you need to earn it!

It was three o'clock in the morning. When he awoke, he wrote again, this time did not cry, he was sure that someone listened to his prayers as he wrote. The title seemed like a contradiction but it was not.

"ALL AND NOTHING"

"There are some things in life

that we should know before birth.
Born knowing, would make sense
to die without knowing anything,
or to live knowing everything.
Everything and nothing at the same time,
that is always the dilemma.
Today I deserve it all and I expect nothing,
or is that I hope all without deserving it?
Everything and nothing are what I want.
I would like to live with everything
and die with nothing
or to live with nothing
and die with everything.
Today I decided to lose everything
because I'll gain everything if I lose it.
Everything and nothing are what I want...
I will love her always on the other side of the wall,
despite my destiny..."

When he finished writing, he lay down again. This time Miel appeared and said in a tone of hope:

—Jacob, it won't be long, you're almost there, don't be discouraged. The tempter will come looking for you soon, don't be fooled. You made an honest inventory of yourself; I was your witness. Saw many of your faults, you fought for freeing from them, but it was not all removed. Those that remain you'll see them, when faced with death.

That night, the owl perched on the edge of his window, turned his back in an act of contempt, then turning his head, rebuked him with mockery.

—Enough with so much suffering! Why don't you give up? She's not here to warm your body in the cold hours of the morning, it's your fault she left. You never loved her, just took advantage of her. She instead loved you like no one else ever did;

you hurt her with a spear at the centre of her heart. You have no forgiveness! You will have to pay for it and give account at the time of your death.

—Shut up, and go! Isn't enough to look at the suffering and loneliness I feel?

—No, I'm never tired to torment those who can't love or forgot about it along the way.

—I don't know what you mean. I still love her...

—If you love her you would still be with her now. How clumsy you are, your prayers never helped you! If you serve me, I'll bring her back.

—No, I prefer to love her in silence without violating my principles. I only have one to whom I owe everything and that is not you. Now go, I want to stay alone with my tears bathed in her memory.

The owl glared at him, turning his head, and flew up toward the top of the oak tree. He still had three days. Its experience told him it would be easy to beat him, it knew his weaknesses and only it had to wait for the right moment. Men with feelings like his were easy to overcome.

Santiago Martinez Concha

XI

The afternoon Crystal met the woman in the ad that looked like her, she lived with her parents she wasn't blind and she saw the world dressed in colours. Years later returned with Jacob to the same place. The ad was still there, perhaps a little discoloured, worn out by time and weather. That was the day she heard the story of 'Burnt House'. They were celebrating one year from the day they first met. Emotions huddled in her throat in a knot, like an eagle's nest, and memories began to flow in a spiral that made her almost impossible to breathe.

In the solitude of the kitchen she continued to collect the flowers from the altar of her memory. That day when she woke up stretched her arms, gently touched his body and stuck to it. That Sunday, after making love, she went to the mountain looking for the smiling woman portrayed at one side of the road. In spite of her blindness in her memory could recognize every turn of the road. When they arrived, they sat down to rest. She felt the shadow of the woman in the ad with white teeth and blue eyes like hers and remembered the sand where she lay and was transported to the magical world of a beach lost somewhere where the sun never hid. She felt a great peace and the desire to stay there and die. Death was not so bad. She had often thought of it. Then asked it for a wish: for a moment to see the colours of the world the way it was, and somehow, she was sure her wish would be granted.

It was on that Sunday when both were fortunate enough to meet Jose Antonio in a bend of the road. Both went to his ranch on a side of the mountain covered with blue grass. On their way back they reached again the woman in the ad and decided to stay there for a while. They loved each other intensely in the cold of the mountain, on a bed of moss, covered with March's stars, Orion in the centre and below, a comet diluted as a splash of milk was lost in the sky below the Pleiades, the dark throne of the Creator.

In the solitude of her kitchen, her soul in tatters, it was like a balm to remember Jose Antonio. A simple mountain's man, wind's philosopher, woods' lover, seasons' sage, sunrise's worker, that had seen them all in seventy years. It was a strike of fate to meet him. When they did at the turn of the road, he was riding on a white donkey stained with grey. The poncho and the hat were also grey. It was five o'clock in the afternoon and the cold wind that blew up put a spiky skin in the back of the donkey and José Antonio was forced to put his hand on his hat to prevent it to fly.

Jacob was the one who took the initiative and spoke first.

—Good afternoon. ¿Are you from around here?

—Yes sir, I was born right here behind those trees, where you see a green light above the field of daisies, beyond those pines, all that green light that reaches the forest. The forest is also mine. There are not many forests like that left around here, you can hear the water running, dripping from every leaf and can breathe fresh air.

—I can imagine it...

—It's better not to imagine it, but to feel it. If you want, we can go there, it's not that far away.

That was how they met Jose Antonio; he had grey watery eyes and bruised hands from the cold. His 'poncho' was damp and his eyes had the vigour of the moor. They hurried to get to his ranch; the sun could barely be seen behind the hills and the increasingly pervasive cold, cut his face on every corner. When they reached José Antonio's birthplace, the afternoon was like a silver tray. A foggy wind began sweeping the grasslands, and then he spoke with pride:

—Here is where my mother was saved from the fire over thirty years ago. Someone whom she didn't know burned the house. So, this site is called *"Burnt House"*. They say that he did it for political reasons but I think it was jealousy. You see, my father never married my mother, but loved her to his death. He didn't leave us his name but left us this parcel of earth. They say that my mother was loved by another that was not my father, but we are my father's children and not the other's. Anyway, whatever they say, the fact was that the house we lived was burned to avenge my mother. Imagine, my mother had eleven children, rest in peace, when he burned the house, but as every cloud has a silver lining, when my father, who rest in peace, learned of the fire, decided to take revenge on the other and let all this land as an inheritance to my mother. Consequently, we now have the land and the memory of my father.

— And… the other?

—Well, they say the other was lost forever. Upon hearing the good my mother's good fortune, decided to hang from the first tall tree he found in his despair. Yes, sir, it was a story of jealousy, the kind that people around here don't forget. My brother Marcus Aurelius was the first to see the dead and ran to tell my mother. I never knew what she thought at the time. She pursed her lips and didn't ask where or how. Since then, I learned not to ask questions at the wrong time.

When they reached the house where Jose Antonio lived, Marcus Aurelius, his older brother was waiting beside Clementine, his wife. Somewhere, Marcus Aurelius planted nine lofty pines that silhouetted against the horizon. When the fog enveloped them, they seemed the guardian angels of the nine circles of heaven.

Her memories were covered by the fog. In the midst of the solitude and silence that enveloped her, Crystal began to forge a decision. She wouldn't suffer anymore because of men. Considered several options, including entering a convent and devote to prayer. The smell of burning candles and the scent of sticky incense, she always liked. Could sing and help in the kitchen or perhaps help the nuns with their laundry. Her mother did the same when she was young and spoke of the immense pond, drilled in a single stone, covered with green moss grown for centuries. The white vestments of the monks reflecting on the still water like ghosts hanging from a rope.

Soon abandoned those ideas, who would want a blind? She thought of running to Jacob's house asking begging him to come back, but knew that was impossible. He was a man of principles and once he made a decision, never looked back. She'd learned to do the same. Considered suicide, but were a believer and the prospect of spending an eternity in hell was terrifying.

—So much pain! She exclaimed—. And… for what?

But in her heart wanted nothing but to recover the man of her life, her memory was tied to him, as the woman of the ad was tied to the fence one side of the road, a destiny which she couldn't escape. Without further thought, felt the need to go back there and feel the cool mountain wind. The next morning, got up early, at five o'clock. The sun had not yet risen. She tore the last page of the book of recipes, and asked the angel of death to grant her wish. She scribbled on the back page, behind the floating island dessert, a note for mother Sabrina, the superior of the Claritas' convent:

"I loved him with the love of a hopeful girl, of a grateful woman. He taught me everything from everywhere, from the top of a volcano, at the edge of the sea or a waterfall, from the

mountain that hides my dreams far away. I have no more words, he took them all, his are already mine ..."

She knocked on the door of the convent. Sarcasm at her side, it ears down and seemed to sense that this was the last time to be with her. The concierge, a novice of smooth braids and light blue habit, recognized her and asked why he was there at dawn. She, with a distant smile that tried to disguise her face haggard with grief, asked her to deliver the last page of the book of recipes to mother Sabrina, to take care of Sarcasm and pray for her. Then, turning round she left.

Crystal and Sabrina shared a secret no one knew. When Crystal arrived one morning at the convent with an old suitcase without having eaten for three days, mother Sabrina, with huge black eyes hidden behind glasses and a huge cap covering her head, opened the door and marvelled with her beauty and in an instant read her soul like an open letter. She asked what she wanted there and she just gave her an answer: 'be myself'. In the following days their friendship strengthened nurtured by kindness and the secret the two began to share.

The day Crystal opened her heart shared with Sabrina the meeting she had with Jacob, the singer who spoke all languages and whose touch healed the wounds, Sabrina began to tremble. She remembered what it was like to be loved and touched by him. Always wondered why he left. At one stage in his youth met him, loving him intensely. Crystal almost couldn't believe her words and cried.

—It's the same man! Then she asked Sabrina how was her face. She told her that her hair was coloured jet black and her eyes were also black. She took off her huge cap, kept her glasses and asked Crystal to tour the face with the tips of her fingers, then she exclaimed with joy:

—How beautiful you are, have a thinner skin than

silk! Then the nun, amid tears confessed her deepest secret.

—My name is not Sabrina... is... Samira, I have gypsy blood... my skin is the colour of cinnamon. If my tribe discover I'm here I would be killed, or if the other novices discover my background, they would arm such a scandal that the bishop would get shoved me. Please do not tell anyone. Many years ago, I came to this monastery and since then I did all the work they asked for. Slowly I gained the confidence of the former superior who entrusted me with various trades, as she was about to die, she told her confessor, a cardinal, I was the one to inherit her post. That's my story on this site.

When Jacob left me, I was depressed, sad and never laugh again. Thinking I was going to die one day I left my tribe and I looked elsewhere. When I came here, I pretended to be an orphan, in a way I was. The superior took me and I decided to be as close to her as I could be. When I met Jacob, he had no more than fifteen years, I too, played with love as a fad, and we were very irresponsible. He had many gifts, he could communicate with birds and spoke all languages, but he suffered a change, perhaps his heart was hardened.

—Celestial heavens! You're beautiful, with reason he chose you, what I don't understand is why he abandoned you...

—Perhaps for the same reasons he left you. ¿He forgot what love was and if he knew he preferred to change it for his principles... and why did he leave you? What were his reasons at that time?

—Maybe he thought he loved me but soon discovered that he didn't. I think so far, he doesn't know what true love is. All started badly. I had a twin sister with dark hair and dark eyes that looked like me. Her name was Sahay. She was murdered along with her daughter because of me. ¡I shouldn't have insisted Rish to come live with us!

—Rish?

—Yes, that's how we called him. To be part of our

tribe, Tlosh, our father demanded he accepted a duel to death with my former fiancé. It's a gypsy love story too complicated for the outsiders. Rish, with the help of the birds defeated Yabor and spared his life, but this act only added further humiliation and shame on him. Yabor married my sister as a vendetta against me, but something else happened. Sahay had a daughter whom she named Fatima, her features were the same as Rish's and the whole tribe made fun of her husband, Yabor then decided murdering both. One night someone heard him utter the gypsy curse while preparing a deadly potion to be mixed with food. We gypsies have secrets that come from ancient times.

In Enoch's Book of Giants, the prophet speaks of the two hundred demons that inhabited the earth before humans. They were divided into twelve tribes and each had a boss. These fallen spirits made a pact. They took as many women each wanted, had children with them and these were the great heroes of old, men of renown and that is what the Holy Book says. The earth was corrupted as well as all flesh and this attracted God's wrath and sent the Great Flood. Each tribe was corrupted. One of them was commanded to teach women to develop secret concoctions and potions and to use exotic makeup to seduce men, ancient traditions tell that gypsies come from them and that our language has older words than those of Sanskrit.

Well, that night after dinner, Yabor fled the camp never to return. Next morning Sahay and Fatima were found dead, but a gypsy never forgets, eventually Yabor will find Rish and kill him and that's what I can tell you. By then I had fled from the tribe and was living in the convent where I adopted the religion I now profess. I live in obedience to secretly purge my sins against love. When Rish comes to the convent I still feel like the first time, my heart cries without anyone knowing and I hide my tears, but now you know everything, I could no longer live without sharing my secret.

Since then they felt part of one another, the continuation of the same. Sabrina had been at the beginning of his adult life and now Crystal at the end. He didn't know that Sabrina was Samira and also never heard that she was the superior of the Claritas' convent. It was written since eternity, but fate's invisible chess was on the table. It was still to be seen who would win God's game.

With her last cents Crystal rented a car, asked the driver to take her to the place in the mountain where the woman of the ad was. She was anxious to get there. The man never knew she was blind. On arrival she gave him the amount agreed and cordially dismissed him. It was noon. The car returned in a cloud of dust. She felt the cool cast by the ad's shadow, looked for the moss' bed, lay facing the sun and fell asleep. Suddenly she heard a noise. The wind brought the sound of a voice like a cataract.

—I'm Miel, the one with a sword. Open your eyes and look at the sun. Now tell me what you see!

She obeyed the command and was shocked to see a being with two eyes like shining drops of honey floating in the air with the sun behind him. He held in his right hand a spear and in the other a steel helmet with veneers also in gold. Her red hair, shining like fire moved this time with the mountain wind.

—I can see you—! She replied embezzled—. Shining like the sun! Below I see the windswept grasslands shine and a playful stream rolling down the mountain—. Raising her eyes saw the woman in the ad with her white teeth and the golden beach of her faraway dreams. She had been granted her last wish.

When mother Sabrina came to look for Jacob, his class was over. He was preparing for the next and final in the morning.

—Crystal is gone—, she said anguished—. ¡I fear for her life and that something may have happened to her, she left me the last page of the cookbook… Take it!

He felt his heart beat like the blows of a battering

ram. The hours that followed were for both a sea of distress. Anything could happen. They searched everywhere, went to the places she used to go but no one had seen her or knew her whereabouts. The only clue was written in the cookbook's leaf in the words that said: "…From the mountain that hides my dreams…" Then in his heart he knew where to find her, she'd be under the shadow casted by the ad's woman, in the same place where they loved each other under a sky of glittering March's stars, refuge from their distant dreams.

Without losing a second both climbed in his old car and he drove desperately towards the mountain. He knew this time was about to lose her beloved forever. They passed by the cloister to pick up the monk, told him the facts, and in a rush all three went in her search, hoping for the best and fearing the worst. No one spoke on the way, each locked in his own thoughts. When they reached the site where the ad's woman was all descended from the vehicle and ran. Jacob asked them to keep a distance, he took off his shoes, walked slowly up to where Crystal' body was, lying among mosses surrounded by orchids and mount ferns. He watched her for a long time without moving a muscle. A strange smile she had never seen before lit her face. The palms of her hands and her eyes were opened facing the sun and a rose lay on her chest and he knew it was meant for him.

Suddenly they all saw Joseph Anthony, Marcus Aurelius and Clementine, coming down the mountain on his white—grey spotted donkey and Jacob told them what'd happened. Jose Antonio to see a flash of light decided to investigate in case it was another fire. That's why they were there this time. Everyone agreed it was a miracle and decided to bury her in secret at the site, below the woman's ad with white teeth and dreams of distant shores. Jacob closed his eyes, took one of her hands in his and kissed her one last time. Her lips were cold and a smell of roses emanated from her body. Sabrina kissed her forehead and eyes, the monk blessed her and her words reminded Jacob of those spoken by the preacher many years ago during the funeral of the teacher: *"Today is holiday in heaven, a servant entered the abodes of love ..."* Clementine gave the wooden chest that had inherited from his aunt and had escaped from burning the night of the fire, Jose Antonio dug the grave, Marco Aurelio made a wooden cross carved with his knife entering Crystal's name and a date: it was a May 5th. A short epitaph said:

> *"Here lies the queen of illusions,*
> *one that lit up the hearts with pure emotions,*
> *and one who knew how to love with no conditions,*
> *and which at the end reached her own conclusions"*

Jacob didn't have much time left or so he felt. He wanted to say goodbye to his children and students. When he addressed his class that morning he spoke of Octavio Paz and asked his pupils to write a poem, could be short or long so far, they'd pass it through the filter of the heart or guts. He said he was reaching its destination and was somehow closing the circle of his own life. Soon they would see him no more. His poems, like his life was coming to an end. He asked them to measure the weight and value of words before writing them or when they thought about them. He remembered what a wise man once told him: *"Poetry is one composed of beautiful words in perfect order."* Then Dalila challenged him defiantly:

—Why don't you write one that everyone can remember?

—He, taking a green chalk, wrote:

> *"This one*
> *I've been asked to write.*
> *Come and gone*

on the same track
wagons loaded
with celebrations
from the heart
carrying old things
and emotions
from the past
with angels bringing
in their hands
the broken
and lost years
gone and come
from places lost
with celebrations
and old tears
from the heart."

—Where will you go—? Asked Dalila.

—To comply with myself! I must leave, now it's time to continue my way alone to discover who I am and what is expected from me.

That night, the blue-eyed angel with large wings began to send him back in time. He saw how his disaffections grew. If one side his life was safe in Vincent's wagon, on the other he had no friends his age and spoke only to birds. He's only eight years, when time came to prepare for his first confession and his father was commissioned to help him. He had to attend sermons on Sundays in the church of a neighbouring town. In one occasion the preacher, an Augustinian monk, focused on the horrors of hell and what it meant to go there. Jacob was so scared that escaped the church and never wanted to return. He did not whistle for several days, hated the preacher and his father for having taken him there. At the direction of the blue-eyed being decided to forgive them both and felt how a heavy burden vanished from his past.

The angel refused to move until he forgave his father for dying and his mother for the same reason. He had been left an orphan and the orphans and the helpless, somehow had marked all of his life. He decided also to forgive all those who caused him any harm. He realized that to Sabrina and Crystal he had nothing to forgive and the last on his list was himself for being so blind. That night in his dream he saw again the being with his huge white-feathered wings wearing a white robe that barely let him see his feet, tied at the waist with a blue streak, her golden hair shone in the moon light in a strange way, his voice was sweet with a serious overtone at the same time. He concluded that this was his guardian angel. He had something of his father and his mother. He looked at him with his huge blue eyes and then said in a friendly and compassionate way.

—It's time to start removing every last one of the masks that hide you from being yourself. Once you do, you'll discover the hidden child abused and afraid that lives in you. You can call me anytime and I'll in your help.

Then he wrote again in the last pages of his notebook still clean:

'If at the end of this trip I discover who I am and learn to laugh at myself without fear of confronting all the pain and fear of my own existence, I'll have reached the top of my own mountain and from there I'll see all the beauty or bitterness that exists when I possess them. '

That would be a journey involving great risks. By removing each mask that hid him from himself, he'd undress a little more. His luggage would be lighter, so light that ultimately, he'd belong to time and find the reason for his existence. Suddenly he began experiencing rapid and profound changes with the loosing of each mask. Between echoes heard words coming from his childhood and recognized his father's: Only those who become like children can enter in heaven.

He read and reread at four years of age the five thick volumes of Calleja's tales, with silvery pages interspersed with narratives. The touch of it reminded him of the brightness of stars and made him dream. With them he came in contact with the world of illusions. Fairy tales taught him that everything was possible to be imagined even eternity as long as he thought about it.

The mask of the hero he invented it along the way. If he was brave or not, he was still to be found out. Sometimes he thought he was and sometimes he wasn't. He'd tried to be. The time he was brave was nothing more than a reflection of his false pride. Sometimes he confused the mask of the hero with that of the brave. Moreover, it was difficult to distinguish between the mask of the hero and that of the martyr. He always admired the martyrs more than the heroes. The martyrs were always in the stories of his childhood with an inexorable end, quickly reaching heaven. Heroes didn't. Every martyr was a hero but not otherwise. Somehow the extreme bloody painful end of the martyrs led the heroes to emulate them and therefore always thought the fastest way to get to heaven was that of martyrdom. To give his life for another, always seemed to him the most courageous act of any human being. Definitely, as child he was convinced that martyrdom was a practical tool that could eventually be used by a coward or a fool like him. He thought that with it, he would get the maximum medal: eternal life in the ninth circle of Heavens! The reverse of the brave's mask was the perfect mould to make him the champion of lost causes, or the perfect idiot. Over time the mould hardened and would hide a tender and vulnerable being, ready to die for his beliefs. As a child he thought it was better to believe in something than not to believe in anything.

The blue-eyed being did not lose a single opportunity taking him back in time, so he could complete an honest inventory of himself. It'd be painful, but essential to find out who he really was. The promise of a happy destiny depended on it. He saw himself at the age of six filled with excitement the day his father came to tell him of the miracle. Gutierrez was a humble village lost in the mountains, one of those sites that do not exist unless a miracle confirms it. It had no access by road and was barely indicated by a dot on any map, but suddenly became for him the centre of the world. There, in the village, hidden in the fog and the immensity of the wilderness, extraordinary things were happening that could move the heart and curiosity of the incredulous. Two children were receiving instructions and heavenly messages to be handed over to the parish priest of the place. When the priest interviewed the older did not believe what he heard. Then he asked the youngest that was not more than five years what was he keeping in his hands. His fists clenched, knuckles white, hardened by the cold and when the priest ordered him to open them, he could not. Then the priest, out of curiosity forced them to open, buy to his surprise, out of the hands of that child, rays of light flooded the room.

Vincent's curiosity prompted him to organize a trip to the site and left in his wagon ready to establish a contact with the life beyond. A week later, both returned from the trip with a happy expression on their faces and a story to tell. Never forgot the smile of the smallest child on whom stood on his shoulders and the tip of the peasant felt hat three sparrows of that wild moor. He thanked his father for taking him there; he'd never met anyone like him and from that day on, he didn't feel so alone. He realized his blessing and that one day he'd have to account for it.

In his dream other years passed like lightning. The smell of burned eucalyptus leaves brought the wet land. He was four years of age running by the mosses, ferns of the field, on a carpet of clover, but that view did not last long. He recalled when some village children mocked him to not be as agile as them. They were all crossing a river, leaping over the stones, to do so, they left him behind and he could not reach them. The soles of his leather boots were slippery when wet and he became paralyzed from fear of falling in the river and remained on one of the stones. He still could not swim, he thought he would drown if he fell into the water being dragged by the current. He cried. After a long time to mourn, returned to shore. The angel stopped there briefly. He could never forgive any of those who committed to him that act of abandonment. He decided to do so at that moment and also forgave them for making fun of him. He could understand then, how rejection was one of his deepest primal fears as why the mask of despair, hatred, indifference and anger had some of those roots. The adventure was bearing fruit and the angel seemed to be satisfied.

That night the angel had prepared him another surprise. He took him in his arms, quickly travelled by all his veins and arteries and visited all his body's organs. Suddenly he stopped in his right leg. The bones presented old scars. He saw himself at the age of three wearing, shorts, brown boots and dirty hands. At that age, his father showed him a short stories' book and offered to give it to him for his birthday. Unfortunately, when he was reciting some Machado's verses in exchange for something to eat, the accident happened. Jacob fell off the edge of the cart and broke his right leg in three parts causing him great pain. Their whistles and tears alerted Vincent who, without missing a beat, took him to a neighbouring hospital. But the worst and the best were yet to come. The doctor who saw him ordered X—rays and ended up plastering both legs, putting a spacer in between his two limbs. He was turned into a sort of "A" letter, the greatest torture for a child being three years old. He could not move or sit and could only lie on his back. So, he spent the three longer months of his life, his legs forming the first letter of his name and the alphabet's.

That was the first time he heard the mention of saints,

when he was a child and his father approached his bed at night, and told him stories, among them the one of his great-grandmother, Beatrice, the one whose tongue was fresh when unearthed to be placed in a crypt and one which according to his confessor, never heard her say a mortal sin. She was young and very beautiful when she met her husband, a General of three suns that was twice her age. And so, with the stories and the voice he loved so much, he fell asleep dreaming with his great—grandmother, whom his father said was holy and people prayed novenas asking her some grace.

Many years later, when he was famous, he was invited to a farewell party for a relative who had decided to leave his job as a banker and become a genealogist. It was at this event, that a fat, bald, red—cheeked man approached him in the midst of two hundred guests, placed a hand to his coat pocket and handed him a thick envelope saying with emotion:

—I've been looking for someone with your profile, you must be a descendant of Beatrice, have the air, tonight, when you get home, go to your studio and open this envelope, it has to do with her and with you too"—. Not out of his surprise, nodded and then the fat man spoke again, this time with a tone surrounded by mystery:

—When I was young, I had a dream one night. I was presented with a woman in a sad voice, dressed in white, with a very thin veil covering her face. When she pulled away the veil, there appeared a very beautiful face with tears in her eyes and then she spoke like this: "My name is Beatrice. Go to the plaza. At the corner where today stands a bank, you will see an old house. Enter in it, in the courtyard you'll find a fountain topped by three bronze herons. In front of the sculpture, under an arch, you'll see a large stone slab on which the water falls when it rains. Lift up the slab and you will find my husband. It is very cold and the poor man has been alone for many years. Pick up his bones, go to the cemetery, find an empty tomb marked with the number '44', I'm buried under the number '43' and put the bones next to mine. In return for your kindness I will grant both wishes you have kept secretly for so long, but remember, once you get them, your only purpose should be: think of the poor and do well! Then I woke up. Not knowing who the woman of my dream was, I ran to find a midwife who knows everybody in town. She's awed to listen to my story, opened an old photo album and asked me to look inside. There were all the notables of the place. Men with moustaches wearing military hats, women in wide skirts suffocated by corsets, three girls dressed in sailor dresses with big black bows on their heads, two midwives, one petting a Persian cat and one with a collar of pearls that reached to the navel, two men with riding boots beside their horses, the photo of a farm known as the Carmen's Mills in the Valley of the Joys and suddenly, when turning the page, I saw her! Excited, I pointed the finger and told the midwife. She's the one! She has the same dress I saw her with in my dream! Then the midwife exclaimed. 'That's Beatrice and that's the dress she wore the day she married. The man behind her is her husband the General'.

—Without further thought—, continued the man with red cheeks, —I went to the bank and told my dream to the manager. He was incredulous, but we went to the yard and found the slabs under the arch, facing the fountain topped by three herons. From there, in his company and his secretary's we went to the police station. On arrival I told my dream back to the lieutenant that served as commissioner. The man then asked two subordinates and the secretary of the inspection to call the coroner and sent for a worker with a spade and a crowbar. At that time, half of the town's people whispered that something strange was going on and hoping to unearth a hidden treasure, joined the procession towards the house where the bank operated. The village priest was not long in coming. His niece, the manager's secretary warned him. The worker took the iron bar and with great effort lift up the slab.

The long white bones of a left hand emerged from the

sleeves of a blue uniform with gold embroidery, grabbing a sword sheathed in its scabbard and engraved with a name. A perfect teeth skull showed the smile of death. The skull wore a hat in the style of the French militia, showing three gold suns in the centre. The bones of the right hand clutched a silver cross on his chest, which had sunk with the weight of years, leaving its mark. The leg bones were into dark blue pants with wide ribbons embroidered in gold, like the buttons on his jacket, and his feet still wore his best black shoes imported from France. He was buried dressed with his uniform, the same he used on the great ball to celebrate the turn of the century—. The man with red cheeks continued with enthusiasm: —We went to the cemetery, found the empty tomb marked with the number '44', after a few prayers and blessings for the General, there he ended up, next to his wife's tomb marked with the number "43".

—I was a student of law school at the time—, continued the fat, red cheeks man, —poor and destitute. One of my secret dreams was to become one-day mayor of my town, the other, governor of the province. After two months of having moved the General's body to his new grave, something happened. The mayor was dismissed for budget mismanagement. He'd kept for his personal use the resources allocated to an orphanage. As there was nobody to replace him someone suggested my name and to my surprise, I was appointed mayor. I remembered Beatrice's words. The first thing I did was ordering to build the orphanage. Two years passed. When I finished my term, the people suggested my name to become provincial governor, a position I still flaunt because I was faithful to my dream. Since then I started to find out more about Beatrice and there were many things I discovered, some of which are in the envelope. I hope you'll enjoy my findings.

That night Jacob met the other half of his ancestors and understood the struggle he'd have to fight. The blue eyes angel was still there watching him patiently. He continued to hear his father's voice as a child telling him bedtime stories. The issue of Beatrice's fresh tong after many years of being dead, always intrigued him, but that night he understood why. The angel showed him his great—grandmother preparing a soup kitchen to feed once a day twenty poor people. She ordered the cars out of the garage of the ranch house where she lived and instead placed a large wooden table and twenty seats. No poor was left without their livelihood at least once a day. The General accepted his wife's initiatives and pleased her in all he could.

The century's turn came and he organized a great festivity to celebrate the event. He invited over two hundred people to their home to a dance that the town would never forget.

Beatriz was dressed with the help of a seamstress who loved her for her kindness. The General had commissioned with great anticipation for that day a surprise coming from Spain. It came in a box lined in ivory silk, tied with a red ribbon to form a rose. When Beatrice opened it, she found a huge 'shawl' and the seamstress exclaimed with sincere admiration:

—Oh, if I had one like that, I would be the happiest woman in the world!

The Beatrice took a pair of scissors and cut it in two.

—Take half, I'll take the other half, my husband has never seen it and no one will ever notice. I hope that makes you the happiest woman in the world!

That night she was splendid wrapped in half shawl and when she went into the yard, all admired it. The General was dressed in his uniform, the same he carried the day he was buried. Beatrice was deeply saddened when he died a short time after. So deep was her grief that she knew her end was near. A year after burying her husband, gathered her three young children and hugging them said with profound emotion:

"I have no more time with you, remember what I say:
Be charitable and always trust God."

She was thirty-three years old when she died, the age at which many saints die. The day of her funeral twenty poor prevented her body to be carried in a hearse. Instead, they loaded the coffin to the cemetery. On the way, three grey herons circled over the funeral entourage until the body was buried. It was as a strange coincidence: May 5th. Then the angel whispered in his ear:

—Don't forget the great lesson Beatrice taught you and practice it! Charity is the key! You still have time, let go of everything and give it to the needy. Don't go the way of the monk who saved the gold coin and was buried with her. Then he remembered when his father gave him a brilliant plated medallion. When Jacob asked him what it was, Vincent replied:

—He's your guardian angel and you should thank him to be alive!

He did not understand very well why he had to be grateful, as it would have been easier if the angel had prevented him from breaking his leg. Only years later he understood that angels do not act like that. It was necessary to break his leg; otherwise his father would have never given the locket with his picture and might not have ever known him. It was difficult to see the image's details. Some things were easier to distinguish than others. He soon discovered that the wings had to be larger than those of the blue and yellow butterflies flying around the field and that he was taller than him. He wore a robe quite comfortable, old—fashioned, attached by a sort of ribbon around the waist. Her hair was also longer than his, his head slightly bent sideways in a compassionate and vigilant way.

He grew and his father always spoke to him with sentences full of mystery. *"Just do what your conscience tells you to do"* was one of those sentences incomprehensible to a child of his age. Why it was born with a mission and strange gifts it was very intriguing. Who would care to look at a child with scratched knees, dirty hands and restless mind? It was difficult to understand what Vincent wanted from him because he loved him while he commanded respect and sometimes fear.

Again, the angel took him back in time until the moment of his birth. He felt when the bubble started to lose water and heard the loud voice of his father ordering his mother. He was face down, his mother seemed not to want him more in her womb and intended to expel him out and she did. He shot like a cork and landed in the middle of his father's arms, still attached to an obscure rope that bound him to her. He was certainly lucky not to be dropped. He felt a great fear when he saw daylight for the first time, the sun seeping between the wagon's canvas and when strong hands cut the umbilical cord. He also perceived as Vincent put it in a container placed next to the bed and began to bathe him with a jug of fresh water. That was the first time he felt and intense cold and saw a blue light coming out of his body. A dreadful fear came upon him. He had just entered alone, the world outside, a strange world where his only defence were his lungs to announce with a high—pitched cry accompanied by tears that he was hungry or that something hurt.

With the first rays of dawn the angel was about to end his mission that night. He heard his parent's voices as if in a bottle full of water with bubbles in it. Saw himself as a sperm in a mad race with others like him. Suddenly he saw a kind of huge planet which he would have to reach. It was his mother's egg against whom he would crash and so he did. Nothing could stop that mad rush that would lead him to be born. He felt the force of impact against the egg as if it was an asteroid that crashed into a planet, then he saw a white light, began to split into various cells and they were all him. He got used to hearing his parents' voice. And so, the days went by like lightning, and nothing new happened since he was conceived. His journey ended at the time. He woke up and saw a shadow outside the window; the owl was looking at him with anger. It was about to lose him.

Santiago Martinez Concha

XII

That night Jacob came home tired after a grey day loaded with work; the kind of day required to get the daily bread. In the morning he taught his students the value of trust and compared it to a necklace. The teaching of the 'object lesson' he learned from the readings of a saint who had mysterious appearances of the Lord. It never failed. He borrowed Dalila's necklace and holding it in his right hand called it the ring of confidence and trust. Then he strung in its coloured pieces of paper each with a written word: loyalty, love, hope, happiness, tolerance, honesty, joy, security and faith. Then he showed his students, what happened upon opening the clasp that held them together, all loose pieces of paper were flying in the air and the ring of trust lost its purpose when broken by distrust. To reinsert the papers and reseal the brooch was a difficult task, sometimes impossible.

At the end of class, he felt like going to a bookstore, browse for some books and say goodbye to his favourite writers. He bought a ham sandwich in mustard sauce with black olives, a small bottle of red wine, he went to the park sat under the silvered eucalyptus tree where he was the first day with Crystal and wanted to write in his notebook things he'd like to read to her but had run out of pages and she was not there to listened. All words were of equal value for him, all with a piece of himself and his life hidden there, like the tears that are found in the tissue after rinsing the soul, which after drying are kept secret and although nobody sees them, they stay there for a while, hoping to meet others that sometimes never come.

In the back of the room's shadows saw another of his masks reflected in a gilt—edged Venetian mirror hanging on the wall. He realized it was the same mirror he'd seen in dreams, hanging in antiquary when he had a vision while being into the Stone Vase. A vision he didn't tell anyone and preferred to keep it for him when a gilt—edged antique mirror with several voices resembling those of a chorus spoke from a corner with dissonant tones:

— I look like one you have in your home. Only serves to hide your own masks. Get rid of me as soon as you can and give the proceeds to the poor. The mirror belonged to many people who've left prisoners in me their pride, vanity and misfortunes. It belonged to a woman who murdered her lover in a jealous rage and I was the only witness to what she did. Then I was sold to a general who lost a war because of his stubbornness and pride. One of his sons sold me to a dictator and when he looked his reflection in me before heading out to his military parades could not see his ugliness, falsehood, vanity and arrogance. At his death, his wife hung me up near the house's entrance and all who came to give her their condolences, left hidden inside me feelings of contempt. Over time, the widow increasingly tired of watching her wrinkles, sold me to the owner of the antiquary. In the mirror he could see the mask of a perfectionist, his own mask. Decided to sell it and give away the proceeds to the poor. Never again would walk into an antique shop.

During the vision in his living room, behind the perfectionist's mask, he saw another, one playing with the reflections of the light. It was the collector's mask. He realized those were the last two layers that hid him from the real self and he'd have to remove them. That night he dreamed of a ferryman with two oars in his hands and a hood that hid his face. He presented himself with a strange voice inviting him to die. Then Jacob asked him with distrust:

—Who are you?

—I am the Acheron, the ferryman of death. The Greeks put me that name, but I've had many others. I'm also called Martyia, the spirit of the night, the angel of death, the bridge between shadow and light, which holds the keys of the tunnel, the angel of hope, of the spear... Do you want me to continue? Don't you recognize me? I am also Miel!

—Ah! Apologies, well... it's been a while since I last saw you. This time you look different...

—You're wrong, this day has passed.

—Well, to me seemed like many years.

—I've come to take you.

—Where?

—To the other side, where there is no return.

—My point of view is changing; I don't know if I want to die tonight. Sometimes I've wanted you to take me, but this time I'm not so sure. I also have many names but that does not make me different than what I truly am.

Not knowing if he wanted to die or not and if in the midst of that infinite order that seems to be the cosmos, it might be possible to refuse his invitation? Then he continued with despair:

—I love life; ¡I could not do without it! You promised me nine days; I still have one more to go...

—A strange way of thinking—, replied the Acheron, you changed a lot over the past eight days. I've always invited living things to die: the day and the night, sunrises and sunsets. If it wasn't for me, life would be meaningless. With no time there would be no clocks or clockmakers. The life cycle is the cycle of death. ¿Do you remember anything you lived before birth? Where was your conscience then?

—I don't know, well I'm not sure if I like this dream. ¡I want to wake up!

—You can't, you're dead! Stop thinking about life and then find out that death is not so bad.

—Do you mean that I can never get up? I didn't have time to say goodbye to my children or my friends or to cancel my appointments for the rest of the week and you come with the story that I'm dead and I should be grateful, ¿for your painless invitation while asleep? Don't you realize I didn't have time to synchronize the two watches that I own? I can't tolerate the clocks running forward or fall behind. When going forward steal time to life and when going behind the same happens. The watches are made to mark the present, never the past or the future. All my watches mark the hour at the same time. I have one that at twelve o'clock plays a country's anthem and another that plays the Angelus. Who will give them rope now?

—What a fool you are! Believe that you're dead! What good is time if you already have it all?

— I want to wake up!

— What for?

—Now that Crystal's gone, I think about my watches and many other things.

—You still have two masks; it is necessary to remove them before taking you with me.

At that moment Jacob realized that one of its most serious defects was perfectionism. It was not only proper of the fools but also of the hard—hearted. He saw the mask reflected in the room's mirror. When looking at the back of it, he found a part of his tragedy. His perfectionism was watching. If things did not follow the prescribed order, then he came up his displeasure, giving vent to his intolerance and impatience.

He thought of his students, his own children and how

often suffered for not finding the answer he wanted. He also thought of Dalila and the desire he felt for her, making it a whim, as another piece to add to his collection of beautiful things. Then he saw the collector's mask hiding in the mirror, a mask of those who were never satisfied with what they had, forgetting happiness. Looking at the back of it he found his greed and desire to collect useless things as well as beautiful, none of which could he take in the Acheron's boat. Then he said with conviction:

—You're right, what folly! So many fears and useless thoughts! I've spent a lifetime collecting things, some because they have value and some because they don't, things seen or unseen, beautiful or ugly, of all sizes, widths, highs, colours and textures, things that sound, that are closed or open, moving, shining, smelling, passing or not passing, things to say or not say, a thousand things, flavours, memories, things that remind us of other things and that lead us gently by the hand until I run out of things. Things that are alive or dead that give light or shade, things to love and things to hate, things that when I die will be sold, gifted, inherited, forgotten or lost. Then he saw his father's face in the mirror, he saw him younger than he was at that time and he told him with nostalgia and gratitude:

—I remember a man who taught another how to grow. I thank you for the mirror with carved golden edges. There I could see part of my destiny, my solitude and my own soul. Thanks, dad, for being the one who taught me the value of beauty, the truth good, the stronghold of faith and the love for others… Then he thought of his books' collection, pictures, and that of a mother he'd seen in a painting at the antiquary with three children begging at the entrance of a church, of utensils of all kinds, his 'box of hope', of his collection of coins and remembered the gold coin he gave the poorest in Alfonso's name, the monk who was serving his sin by hiding it. He reviewed his collection of medals, records, ties and old shoes, of shirts he no longer uses and were still kept in a closet. Recalled the day he went to a mountain to visit a peasant woman who was granted with celestial visions. When he reached the shack where she lived, she was smiling and with a sweet smile offered him all she had: a hardened piece of brown sugar and two roasted cobs grown in her yard. He noted that her modest room had no floor, she walked barefoot, and his clothes were in tatters, then he offered his help in a modest way:

—I'll give you money to buy some clay tiles that will form the floor. I'd also buy you some shoes and a new dress—. She looked at him with her sweet smile and answered:

—Thanks, but I can't accept it. The Lord forbade me, he told me that the floor I have is enough. He made it and I can step on it barefoot. Nor am I allowed having more than two changes of clothing, the one I'm wearing and another one which is drying.

Then he thought of an epitaph for his tombstone but did not tell the Acheron, he would write it on a piece of paper and hand it over to the monk next day. He thought again of his life, his collections, and the time he spent doing them and made a decision, if the Acheron permitted, he would give it all to the hospice's children next day. Mother Sabrina would know what to do with it all. He heard again the voice of the Acheron with an echo coming from behind:

—Don't forget to pay me if I take you to the other side. Two coins will suffice. Tell the one who'll bury you to put one above each eye, I will come for them and give it to the poorest.

He realized that there was but one person to forgive and that was himself. He imagined a huge dark scenario where there was no one but him. When the lights lit it, he began to be filled with gratitude and gifts of the spirit. Gratitude for being born and having lived; gratitude was the key to get rid of every weight and of all blame. Then he realized that there were only two ways to be reborn and that they were the same as having a child. First, he had to imagine it in order to have it, and then to have it in order to imagine it. He saw himself dead by a moment, then alive somewhere else. The Acheron's voice reverberated with echoes in his dream:

—Wake up and live a little more if you want. You still don't deserve death. When I re—invite you, I hope you won't mind your watches or your collections, then I can show you other worlds and reveal you my secret, meanwhile, sleep the dream of life, there's still one more day to go.

—Wait, wait… don't go yet! I still have to say goodbye to all those who accompanied me in my long journey while searching for the treasure hidden in the Chest of Life under the roots of the Big Tree. I can't leave without saying goodbye to all of them for their help. It was thanks to their courage and advice that I managed to find much of what I appreciate and value today.

—Here they are. They never left your side. If you happen to need them again, open the Book of Life and search for their names there. When you do, they'll come alive and you'll see them by your side. Now turn to look.

Orok is the first to embrace him, then his wife Queen Ester and their daughter Princess Blue. Then Orok says with a hoarse voice:

—Remember: *"things are not what they appear to be."*

Then the fairies April and May appear, flying over him, and dropping flowers when they sing:

"Sometimes things are not what they seem.
Others they are what they are.
Learn to distinguish the truth from the false;
the real from the unreal,
only you can build the bridge
that'll bring you back to a good life."

Behind them are Sun and Moon, Balm, Malchus, the giants, walrus, Morg, Grom, Ajiela, Nova, Alfonso, the Solitary, the beggar with her children, Jacob, Seraphim, and all the defective released with his words through Miel's help, changing their flaws into virtues, transforming them into humble, modest, friendly, fair, kind, generous and honest, marking the path he should be known.

He woke up this time feeling relaxed. Nothing mattered anymore on this earth after Crystal's death and his dream with the Acheron. The Magical Kingdom of Orok was restored, what he learned with the Chest of Life was given to scientists in a letter that explained how to face the future. He went to the corner by the entrance, to the table where he left his keys, his old hat and umbrella. Above it, decorating the wall as a warning, the clock was playing a hymn. He opened the glass top and took the pendulum mechanism seized with a steel hook. The hands marked 3 am, the dark hour of tribulation. It was his favourite time to pray.

He thought his own hour was at hand and began preparing a will which he'd give it to the monk next day, the day of eclipse. It was not much he'd have to give. Over the years almost everything was gone. The piano he gave it to the Clarita's convent, the notebook to his children, the pen with which he wrote the pieces of his life left it to the monk, his watches to the neighbourhood's school, his old parchment's books and copper medals were to be sold, its product handed with everything else that was not described, to mother Sabrina and the children's hospice, the old carpet he left to Dalila to remind her of their sin and finally, his wide brim brown felt hat to Jose Antonio. The little money he'd saved, should cover the funeral's costs, if possible, his body should be buried in the mountain, under the woman's ad with white teeth and so, armed with his heart in one hand and hope in the other, he decided to face the Acheron next night. Death didn't matter for him anymore and life without Crystal either.

ooo

The morning of his date with destiny he dressed up like his grandfather the General. He wore his last white shirt and midnight blue suit he'd saved for the occasion. He used the colony Crystal liked, with lemon and lime fragrance, reached into his closet where he found his yellow tie with flying swallows and thought of the trainer he'd been. Smiling he went for a walk in the park to say goodbye to the sun. That afternoon he visited his children, after holding them in his arms, blessed them and gave them the last words he'd written for each. To the oldest bearing his name gave him his notebook with a letter folded in four that said:

"Beloved son who I hugged first, watch your primogeniture aiming always to be fair, defend the lost causes, love the poor and weak. Much is expected of you if you meet your inheritance. Received the best I had and the little I knew. Forgive me if I was ever wrong or couldn't do better. To the extent of my imperfections you can be better than me. Watch over your brothers, don't prevent your kids from feeling pain and instead help them to overcome it, teaching them always to trust God.
I love you with my soul, your father,
Jacob
P.S. If you publish my notebook, it belongs to all three."

To his daughter Isabel he gave her gave a box of chocolates, some filled with truffles and others with coffee creamer. In the centre, a red ribbon holding three red roses and a letter folded in four saying:

"Dear daughter, I write to you from the bottom of my heart. You were born the day of the eclipse and with the eclipse I must leave. The first thing I saw was your tiny hands, now I see you as a woman. Of my three children you inherited my enthusiasm and desire to write. Hope you'll do better than me. I always loved you with my soul and expect a lot from you. I know you'll you're your expectations. Do not be afraid when you feel faint. The work you have chosen requires the truth. Love truth, seek truth, defend the truth and the truth will love you seek and defend you. In truth there is a measure of the infinite. He is the truth, beauty and love at the same time. Nothing can ever hurt you if you trust Him.

I love you with my soul, your father,
Jacob"

To his son Ignatius, the youngest of the three, gave him a tender embrace and a small dog with white and brown spots. It'd a happy face like him, with a tail always pointing to heaven, he told him the story of Diogenes the philosopher walking with a flashlight during daylight looking for an honest man. Told him he expected him to be that man and gave the dog that name. Drawing from his pocket the note he'd prepared folded it in four and he gave it to him. Then Ignacio read it in silence, his little hands trembling with emotion. It said like this:

"Dear son, great in my heart. You have been my companion during these years of my life and were the reason for me to live again. Now I must go to a place where you can't still accompany me, but from there, I'll always watch over you. Strive to be happy. I know someday you will come to meet me with your other brothers and by then we will all be in the way of true love. Always trust in God.

I love you with my soul, your father,

Jacob"

Ignatius embraced him with tears in his eyes, he said goodbye, then hugged Diogenes and ran after him. His father knew he'd be a happy child. Writing to his children freed him from all fetters from the past. He understood the importance of doing it and gave thanks. The time given to him was enough for. Nothing was left to hazard, he's ready to go.

Jacob didn't sleep at home. Instead he asked the monk if he could stay in the cloister his last night. Together they saw the moon hiding at midnight. Crystal, before watching the sun die on the mountain had prepared the children's hospice with dances and songs written by him for that party of "burning fires". The hospice was adjacent to the convent and the woods in between them were crowned by the old oak. It was a night of cold noses, with a moon so big that everyone thought it was going to explode. That was the night the shadow of the earth tore a bite to the moon, in which summer began and came with the dry wind coming from the mountain, the moon twice dressed in white till midnight and in yellow until dawn.

That was the night of light and shadow, as he wrote to mark the eclipse, one in which Crystal became blind, before he knew her. For many years everything was there in his notebook. The day of that eclipse also his daughter Elizabeth was born. He wrote a poem on the occasion of that clear night when she first saw the moon like a fairy trying to catch it with her tiny hands. That was the night the fairies came out of their cocoons and spread their wings of white light throughout the forest and the elves left their secret caves beneath the oak and danced under the fern forests, singing in chorus with the children a ballad that it said:

"Tonight, is the night; ¡the day has come!
If you don't believe come out and mourn!
Today is the feast of the great full moon

If you do believe won't feel the pain,
If you don't believe will feel ashamed
go out and seek, and you'll see the moon,
now are together night and day.
Tonight, is the night; ¡the day has come!
If you don't believe come out and mourn."

He heard Crystal's voice like a whisper brought by the breeze coming from the forest and he felt goose bumps.

—Jacob, Jacob, where are you? ¿Are you cold? Come with me my beloved, I'll warm you up with my body.

That night of light and shade, the forest was filled with scents of hidden mosses that awoke with the moon and dew fell from heaven and stuck to the trees' leaves turning them into glass sculptures. From the forest's clearing came with the rustling of leaves the children's voices singing in unison:

"Tonight, is the night; ¡the day has come!
If want to be loved, I want to be healed.
Tonight, is the night of the sun and moon!
And the earth is to be finally saved.
If you don't believe go out and feel,
the taste of the dew, the smell of the earth.
Today is the day with the whiter night,
when mosses open and shadows flight.
Tonight, is the night, the day has come,
If you don't believe come out and mourn.
Tonight, is the night; ¡the day has arrived!"

The fire lit and warmed the children's faces and hands. He took from his pocket a piece of paper and wrote on it the epitaph which was to be engraved on his tomb and handed it to the monk also with his pen. With this act he closed the last chapter of his life. When the Acheron came, he could go now in peace. It read like this:

"Surrender frees you from the bonds of the past.
Hope emerges when the wreck is sad.
Love forgives, when nothing else exists.
Serenity and acceptance are the keys.
Gratitude conquers if you insist."

Miel's voice pulled him out of that full moon's spell. He came with a serene face when he spoke:

— Tonight, is the night!

—The day has come, are you also the Acheron?

—Yes, don't forget to pay me. Do you have two coins?

—No, I gave it all to the hospice's poor.

— So, how do you intend me to take you across?

—I've got my own boat and two oars.

— And what is the boat made of?

—Life itself. We must be grateful for it.

— And the oars?

—Read my epitaph, when the time comes...

— You're ready! This is the time I waited for. You understand what love is, after losing it! You can ask one last wish.

—No, I want nothing; ¡I had everything and lost it! I didn't value what destiny offered me.

The angel approached him and blew over his body; Jacob felt a gentle breeze and when his soul stripped off from the armour he'd built during many years. He was traveling light.

—It's time to leave.

At that moment the angel turned into water drops and the forest was silent in a quiet instant. Jacob suddenly felt his body planted in the soil with roots penetrating the earth beyond the wet moss. He began to absorb drop by drop the water hidden under the ground and slowly went disintegrating, as part of the skin covering the forest till, he completely disappeared. —I still have my conscience, he thought. At last I am free; I can run like water. I am already a part of this land.

—So is death, Miel answered!

— What about life?

—Life is an illusion in time. We're God's toys.

— And my destination?

—It's still in my hands. I can give it back to you at dawn if you still want it. Henceforth no longer you'll be afraid of death, you can imagine it like water.

—It's true, then, what should I fear?

—Life! You can lose it all if you take the wrong path!

He felt his body absorbed with force and began to slowly evaporate. He was soon turned into a mist that covered the earth and rose slowly through the Eucalyptus's branches.

—It's wonderful, it's better than being alive!

—You're wrong—! Replied the angel… You are alive!

It was when the eclipse ended, he breathed his last. In the midst of a bright moon, he thought he saw Crystal's silhouette surrounded by swallows. She was covered with tiny roses covering her body. Her blue water eyes were on him and her hands spread up to touch him. Her lips parted in a smile that showed white teeth, like those of the women in the announcement, hugged and slowly walked through the mist till they disappeared. That night the owl took refuge in the oak's branches, it was angry and about to lose him, he still had one more day, but there was little it could do now...

XIII

Jacob woke up early in the morning with the light on, the notebook in his hands and Crystal huddled body next to his. The sun streamed through the curtains' fabric stroking her blonde hair, making it shine with every ray of sunshine. He was not sure what'd happened and if it all was just a dream. He reviewed again each piece of the puzzle in his memory: Miel, the nine days, her parents, the gypsy, Simona, Tania, the monk, Dalila, the Tree of Life, the Stone Vase, the group, his character defects, the woman in the ad, Jose Antonio, Marco Aurelio, his students, his children, his past, his love for Crystal. Everything was so real! The bittersweet pain in the chest left by the steel serrated spear was still there. Then he wondered if he was alive. Again, his hands looked for his entrails. At that moment he remembered the words of the angel early in his sleep the first day:

"Open your eyes, listen, things are not always what they seem.
You should ask at every step the reason why and the reason
for your existence. And remember: always trust God"

She was there, still, alive, as a dove resting motionless in his arms. He felt her heart's beating, the warmth sheets, and the rose-scented fragrance emanating from her skin. A strange joy and deep gratitude made him tremble. Both were still part of this world. She took a deep breath, stretched her arms and put them around his neck, then opened her blue eyes as the sea and said in a voice that was not yet fully awake.

— I dreamed with an angel. He gave me nine days to find my destiny. It was a long deep sleep. He took me in his arms in the air. From the top I could see the dry trunk of a huge tree once inhabited by thousands of birds. The angel told me that the tree was you, who like many humans, your roots had dried up because of selfishness and you wouldn't have peace until you find your own water. He also told me that my destiny was tied to yours, we could never separate even if we wanted, that we were part of each other and there was hope, because you had finally forgiven yourself.

— Ready? What for?

—To accept the commitment to love me as I deserve. That he also gave you nine days and that already you knew the way.

Jacob began trembling.

—That's true—, he replied. —I also had a dream, I saw my own life and that you are the water that fills my heart. We will walk together to reach the final destination; we will be together forever. Tell me, will you marry me?

—You know that I do. When?

—Today. God is in a hurry. We can ask the monk to officiate the ceremony and mother Sabrina to act as our witness. I was never so sure. I think there is no time to lose. What else the angel told you?

—That I could recover my sight if we followed his instructions. All you have to do is get a fresh fish in the market, to open it and get its gall and make an ointment with them. With one third you should anoint my eyes tonight. Another third should be placed on a censer with burning coals by way of exorcism and the remaining third must rub on your chest where your heart is in the same place where he went through with his spear. Only this will heal the wounds that you caused others or yourself in the past.

He began to mourn as a child. It was all true, in spite of what happened they were still alive. They had a new opportunity with a new destiny. With humility they went first to the cloister, they met with the monk and told him what happened. The monk understood immediately that a miracle had taken place and explained once again why many of the so called 'marriages' are not from God and he married them without further questioning. He gave them as a wedding present a framed prayer decorated with a flowers garland.

After the ceremony, all three went to the market, they bought a fish and they did what the angel had prescribed. Then the monk prepared an ointment with the fish's gall and after blessing it, applied it to Crystal's eyes, rubbing it on the eye lids. In doing that, the monk performed a millennial exorcism. When she opened her eyes, she saw the afternoon sun for the first time in years. It was equal to the one she had seen with the tips of her fingers and imagined through the eyes of the soul.

Dalila published Jacob's memoirs. After nine months of that afternoon when she was with him, she had a daughter and called her Samira. She spent years collecting his writings until one day she met Crystal, she got the notebook from her with all his scrabbles and together went to the Claritas' convent and met Sabrina. She lent them the little sandal box and when they opened it, a delicious scent emanated from it and there they found the rest of his writings, a tuft of hair, some milk teeth and they could assemble this story. The secret they share is still with them.

MIEL   Santiago Martinez Concha